"Where did this second set of footprints come from?" Erin asked.

Dillon scanned the area around them until he finally pointed to some underbrush. "Based on the direction of the shoe print, I'd say the tracks came from that direction."

Erin followed his point to a rocky outcropping—the perfect place to hide out and wait for someone to pass.

"You think someone abducted Bella, don't you?"

Dillon's gaze said everything even though he didn't say a word. That was exactly what he thought, Erin realized.

She couldn't fall apart. Not now.

She'd have time for that later.

Right now, all her energy needed to be focused on finding Bella.

The group continued walking. They veered off the main trail and into the woods.

Danger seemed to hang in the air at every turn.

Just then, Scout stopped walking and sat at attention.

Erin sucked in a breath.

She knew what that meant.

It meant the K-9 had found something.

Christy Barritt's books have won a Daphne du Maurier Award for Excellence in Suspense and Mystery and have been twice nominated for an RT Reviewers' Choice Best Book Award. She's married to her Prince Charming, a man who thinks she's hilarious—but only when she's not trying to be. Christy is a self-proclaimed klutz, an avid music lover and a road-trip aficionado. For more information, visit her website at christybarritt.com.

Books by Christy Barritt

Love Inspired Suspense

Keeping Guard
The Last Target
Race Against Time
Ricochet
Desperate Measures
Hidden Agenda
Mountain Hideaway
Dark Harbor
Shadow of Suspicion
The Baby Assignment
The Cradle Conspiracy
Trained to Defend
Mountain Survival
Dangerous Mountain Rescue

Visit the Author Profile page at LoveInspired.com.

DANGEROUS MOUNTAIN RESCUE

CHRISTY BARRITT

LOVE INSPIRED SUSPENSE

INSPIRATIONAL ROMANCE

LOVE INSPIRED SUSPENSE
INSPIRATIONAL ROMANCE

ISBN-13: 978-1-335-73604-8

Dangerous Mountain Rescue

Copyright © 2022 by Christy Barritt

This edition published by arrangement with Harlequin Books S.A.

For questions and comments about the quality of this book, please contact us
at CustomerService@Harlequin.com.

Love Inspired
22 Adelaide St. West, 41st Floor
Toronto, Ontario M5H 4E3, Canada
www.LoveInspired.com

Printed in U.S.A.

Who hath delivered us from the power of darkness,
and hath translated us into the kingdom of his dear Son:
In whom we have redemption through his blood,
even the forgiveness of sins.
—*Colossians* 1:13–14

This book is dedicated to the "coffee lobby" gang at church. I'm so thankful for all the laughs, stories and talks!

ONE

"Bella! Can you hear me?"

Erin Lansing paused at the edge of the trail and surveyed the wintery mountain vista in front of her.

She knew her search efforts were most likely futile. She'd already explored this area twice with no luck.

There were still no signs of her daughter anywhere on this mountain.

As she stood at the overlook and caught her breath, investigators were gathering a team to search for Bella. But Erin couldn't wait for them. Their process was too slow. There was too much time to lose, time she couldn't afford to let slip away.

Would law enforcement drag their feet on purpose? Maybe to get revenge on Erin or to show their loyalty to her ex-husband, Liam?

Ever since Liam had disappeared a year ago, she'd been the number-one suspect in the eyes of his colleagues. Just because she and Liam had had a public fight right before he'd vanished didn't mean Erin was guilty.

Liam had been a cop. But instead of looking at people he'd arrested as potential suspects, investigators had focused all their attention on her.

Had the person responsible for her ex-husband's disappearance decided to come after Bella also?

A rock formed in Erin's gut at the thought. She didn't even want to think about it.

All she wanted was to find Bella.

A sixteen-year-old shouldn't be out in this wilderness alone. The vast Pisgah National Forest of North Carolina, with its deep valleys, steep cliffs and wild animals was no place for an amateur. To make matters worse, Bella hadn't taken her anxiety medication with her.

Erin knew how Bella got when she didn't take her medicine.

She would be beside herself. Close to panic. Jittery.

Tears pressed at Erin's eyes as she glanced at the scenic view in front of her one more time.

But there was nothing to indicate Bella had been there. No clues as to what had happened after her daughter had left for school yesterday morning. All she knew was that Bella had never made it to school and that her car had been found at the parking lot near the trailhead.

Bella had never shown any interest in hiking the mountain before. She wouldn't have come out here on purpose, would she?

Erin heaved her backpack up higher and turned to continue down the trail. She'd keep searching until she found Bella. She was even prepared to sleep in this wilderness if that's what it came down to.

But the one thing she wouldn't do was sit back and wait. Not anymore.

The old Erin had been passive. People had walked all over her. But after adopting Bella six years ago, she'd become a new person. A stronger person.

As her phone buzzed, Erin glanced down, surprised to have any reception out here.

The message on her screen made her blood run cold.

You deserve this.

She sucked in a breath.

Who could have sent this?

Someone evil—that was who. Someone who wanted to put Erin in her place. To let her know she was a villain.

Could this person have taken Bella?

A surge of concern and anger tangled together inside her.

This was becoming even more of a nightmare than she'd thought possible.

Quickly, she typed back.

Where is she? What do you want from me?

She waited a few minutes, but there was no response.

Disappointment clutched her, but she pushed it aside. She needed to keep moving.

Erin continued down the narrow trail that cut along the side of the mountain. She sucked in a deep breath, inhaling the vague scent of pine and old leaves left over from the autumn purge.

The trees around her were fragile from the winter. Branches seemed to reach for her, their sharp edges grabbing her hair and jacket. And the air was so cold out here that every breath hurt her lungs.

Was Bella out here somewhere? Was she cold? What had she worn when she'd left for school yesterday? Erin had already left for work, so she didn't know. What about food? Was her daughter hungry?

The questions made Erin's temples pound, made worry swirl in her gut until she wanted to throw up.

She hadn't passed anyone in the two hours since she'd been out here, even though this trail was normally popular, even in the winter months. But today, clouds threatened freezing rain or snow and kept most of the hikers away. Precipitation, thirty-degree temperatures and slippery slopes didn't make for ideal hiking conditions.

Erin heard a stick crack nearby and paused. The hair on her neck rose as she turned.

She scanned the wooded landscape around her but saw no one.

So what had caused that sound? Could it have been an animal?

That made the most sense.

She swallowed hard, trying to push down her fear.

But as she continued walking, her fears escalated, fueled by her imagination.

What if Bella had met somebody online and come here to talk face-to-face? Erin had heard stories about things like that happening. Even though she wanted to believe Bella would never take that risk, she couldn't say with one hundred percent certainty that her daughter wouldn't.

Erin rubbed her temples, wishing she could clear the fog from her head. She needed to be sharp if she was going to hike out here. Distraction could get her killed, especially with the craggy rocks, steep trails and slippery passes coming at her from every angle.

She glanced down, watching her steps as rocks rose and jutted out from the soil on the path. A small stream cut down the side of the mountain and trickled in front of her. The moisture and freezing conditions made every step treacherous.

Just last week, someone had died after slipping off a cliff on one of these trails. The man's death had been all over the news, a grim reminder of how dangerous nature could be.

At the thought, more images of Bella filled Erin's mind and she bit back a cry.

Please, Lord. Watch over her. Please! I'm begging You.

She prayed nothing had happened to her girl. Bella had problems—more than her fair share for someone her age, it seemed. But she didn't deserve this.

Another stick broke in the distance.

Erin's lungs froze as she stopped and turned around.

Somebody else was out here. She felt certain of it.

Glancing ahead, she tried to measure how safe the upcoming section of the trail was. When she'd come this way earlier, she'd turned around before continuing through this section. She'd been afraid to go any farther.

A narrow path stretched against the cliff face. If she continued, this part of the hike would be challenging. Maybe even life-threatening.

But if she turned around to head back, she could be confronted by whoever shadowed her.

As she heard another stick crack, closer this time, Erin knew she only had a few seconds to make a choice.

She let out a long breath. For Bella's sake, she had to persist.

Erin rolled her shoulders back before continuing down the trail. She would need to move quickly but carefully.

She hit the first part of the narrow pass without problems—and without hearing any other mysterious sounds behind her.

Just as she reached the end of the stretch, another noise filled the air.

The sound of heavy footsteps rushing toward her.

As she turned to see what was happening, hands rammed into her back.

Then she began falling down the steep rock face into the valley below.

"I'm going to need you to give this everything you've got, boy." Dillon Walker knelt in front of his dog, Scout, and rubbed his head.

The border collie/St. Bernard mix stared back at him, his soulful brown eyes giving every indication that the canine had understood each word Dillon said. The two of them had worked together uncountable hours in order to reach this level of bonding.

Dillon rose and gripped Scout's lead as they prepared to head down the steep mountain trail stretching beside them. As a brisk winter wind swept around them, Dillon pulled his jacket closer. Scout also had on a thick orange vest with "Search and Rescue" on the side.

The temperature had dipped below freezing, which would make the trails both slippery and treacherous. Those conditions also made it more urgent to find Bella Lansing sooner rather than later.

"I appreciate you coming out here to do this." Park Ranger Rick Manning appeared beside him, his breath frosting as soon as it hit the frigid air. "I know it's been a while and that you gave up this line of work."

Dillon held back a frown. "I'm only doing this as a personal favor to you."

Dillon had been a state police officer for nearly a decade before making a career change two years ago. Now, he trained officers on how to be expert K-9 handlers. He taught others so they wouldn't make the mistakes he had. He lived with guilt every day because of those very oversights.

"I wouldn't have called you if it wasn't for the snowstorm headed this way." Rick nodded toward the gray sky above. "We don't have much time, and you are the best K-9 handler I know."

"Some people might argue that point." Dillon frowned as memories tried to pummel him. Accusations. *Truths.*

"You're the only one who's inclined to

argue." Rick lowered his voice. "No one but Laura blames you for what happened to Masterson, you know."

Dillon didn't acknowledge his friend's words. Instead, he readjusted the straps of the backpack he'd filled with water, protein bars and dog treats. He wanted to be prepared for anything while they were out here.

A team of rangers would accompany Dillon and Scout in their search efforts.

A teen was missing. She was believed to be out here in the vast wilderness of the Pisgah National Forest in western North Carolina, and they needed to find her.

This was what Dillon and Scout had trained to do. The two made a great team.

But whenever Dillon had to utilize his dog in this way, it was never good news.

Not only was the situation precarious because of the missing teenager, but forecasters were calling for snow tomorrow. If Bella was out there, they needed to find her now.

"We're just waiting for Benjamin to show up," Rick said. "I'd like you to take the lead."

Dillon shook his head. "I'm not law enforcement anymore."

"It doesn't matter. You know what you're doing. You know these trails—far better than the rest of us," Rick said.

Thankfully, Benjamin strode up just then, giving Dillon an easy out in the conversation.

Dillon didn't want to be in charge. However, he'd do whatever it took to find this girl.

He glanced behind him at the parking lot. An ambulance waited there. Paramedics needed to be on call in case the team found Bella in an injured state. Dillon hoped that wasn't the case. He hoped the teen was simply lost but unharmed.

Please Lord, give her a happy ending. I can't handle another replay of Masterson.

Masterson was another hiker Dillon had set out to find. Only there hadn't been a happy ending for that search and rescue mission.

Dillon swallowed hard as he focused on the trail ahead.

The woods surrounding him were part of the Blue Ridge Mountains, and people came from all over the East Coast to experience the rolling peaks of the national forest, which boasted several different waterfalls. The area was simply breathtaking, even now at winter's end when the branches were bare.

As Dillon prepared himself to start, a gloved ranger brought a bag over. He held it toward Scout and opened the seal at the top.

Bella's sweatshirt was inside.

Scout took a deep sniff then lifted his nose to the air, trying to find the girl's scent.

Her beat-up Honda Civic had been found in a lot not far from here. This trail seemed the most logical as to where she would be.

Scout tugged at the lead before pulling Dillon along the trailhead into the threadbare forest. As he did, Dillon mentally reviewed the case.

Bella Lansing had been missing for twenty-six hours. She'd left home for school yesterday morning but had never returned, nor had she shown up for classes. The rest of the day had been spent calling friends and searching hangouts.

There had been no leads.

Then a ranger had found her car in the lot

near these woods this morning. That's when the rescue had been organized.

She wasn't an experienced hiker, nor was she familiar with this terrain. According to the report, Bella had never shown any interest in exploring these mountains. She had no survival training, but her winter coat had been missing from the house. Dillon hoped that meant she was wearing it. She'd need it out here in these elements.

Scout's actions indicated the girl had traveled this trail. What Dillon didn't know was if she'd been alone. As one of the more popular hikes in the area, any footprints would have been concealed at this point.

The rangers working the case would figure out the details. Dillon's only job, along with Scout's, was to find Bella.

"You know who Bella's mom is, don't you?" Rick asked quietly as they started down the trail.

Dillon shook his head. "No idea. Honestly, it doesn't matter if she's a criminal or a philanthropist, either way, her daughter deserves to be found."

"I should have expected that reaction from you." Rick shook his head and let out a light chuckle. "You're a good man, Dillon Walker."

He didn't know about that. He only hoped this search didn't end tragically.

These mountains were no place for the inexperienced. He'd seen too many tragedies happen here. Tragedies that had changed people's lives forever.

Just like they'd changed his.

Pushing those thoughts aside, he continued down the path. Scout was on the scent—and that was a good sign. With every minute that passed, Bella's trail could fade with time and the elements.

If Dillon had known the girl was missing earlier, he would have advised the team to start at sunrise. Instead, they'd already wasted a good three hours of daylight.

What had his friend meant when he'd asked if Dillon knew who Bella's mom was? It truly didn't matter to him, but he was curious. When Dillon had been a state cop, he'd been headquartered an hour and a half from this area. He knew little about the small towns dotting these mountains.

They continued down the trail, the miles passing by.

As he reached an area of the hike known as Traveler's Bend, he tugged Scout to a halt.

What was that sound?

"Dillon?" Rick looked at him.

He raised a finger in the air, indicating for everyone to be quiet.

That's when he heard it again.

"Please, help me!" A soft voice floated from below.

Was it Bella? Had they found the girl?

As if Scout sensed something was wrong, the canine began to bark at the edge of the path.

Dillon hurried toward the slippery, rocky cliff and peered down below.

A woman clung to a branch there, terror on her face.

It wasn't Bella. Dillon had seen the girl's picture.

But this woman clearly needed help.

"Stay right there!" he yelled. "We'll get you!"

The woman opened her mouth to speak. But as she did, the rocks beneath her crumbled and she began plummeting to the ground below.

TWO

As Erin felt herself falling, she clung to the
branch she'd been hanging on to, praying
her grip was tight enough to catch her, praying the branch was solid enough to remain
rooted.

Her body jerked to a halt before cascading
to the rocky ground below.

Thank you, Jesus.

Her heart pounded in her ears at the realization of how close she'd come to death—again.

She'd heard voices above her. Or had she
imagined them?

Was someone really there who could help
her? Had the search party caught up with her?
Or was it just simply the person who'd pushed
her?

She continued to grasp the tree branch,

praying her fingers wouldn't slip. Her arm was so tired. She felt so weak.

She tried to look up, but the cliff face jutted out just enough to make it difficult.

"Help me!" she yelled again. Her voice sounded as desperate as she felt.

She tried to take a deep breath in order to yell louder. But her lungs felt frozen.

The position she hung in didn't help. Her body bent, making it hard to get enough air into her system. What air she did pull in was so cold, it nearly took her breath away.

The side of the cliff face was directly in the path of the wind. The icy breeze hit her full-force.

How long would it take for hypothermia to kick in?

Oh, dear Bella... I'm so sorry. It wasn't supposed to turn out this way.

"We're going to help you!" someone yelled above her.

Yes, someone was there!

Someone who sounded like he wanted to help.

Not the person who'd done this to her.

She drew in as deep of a breath as she could. "Help me!" she yelled again. "I'm down here!"

Erin waited, trying to hear a response. But it was no use. The wind muffled the sounds around her.

Had it muffled her voice also?

Despair tried to clutch her, but Erin pushed the emotion away. This was no time for hopelessness. She needed to stay positive.

Just as the thought rushed through her head, a rock crumpled beneath her.

She looked down and saw it tumbling, tumbling, tumbling.

How many feet was it to the bottom?

She couldn't bear to think about it.

She drew in another breath. "I don't know how much longer I can hold on!"

Did the person above her understand the urgency of the situation? What was he doing?

A new sound filled the air.

Was that a…bark?

Erin felt certain that it was.

Maybe help really was here. Maybe this mountain wouldn't be her death.

She'd never meant to draw attention away

from Bella and onto herself. And she wouldn't forgive herself for that.

But she needed to be there for Bella once she was found.

She looked up again, straining her neck as she tried to get a glimpse of what was going on.

A man stared down at her. "We're here to help! Are you hurt?"

That was a good question. Was she hurt?

Maybe she'd cut her leg. She might have some bruises.

But none of that mattered, not if she was alive.

"I'm fine!" she called. "But please hurry."

"We're going to send a rope down to you. I need you to grab it with both hands."

The thought of releasing her lifeline—a tree branch—caused a shot of terror to rush through her. "I… I can't let go."

"We're going to talk you through it, okay? You can do this."

The man's voice sounded so soothing that Erin wanted to believe him. Plus, he'd said "we." Were there more people up there, more than just the man and his dog?

Another surge of hope swelled in her.

Erin had no *choice* but to trust this man.

From what she'd seen, the man wore a black jacket and a stocking cap. Was he a hiker?

As if to answer her question, someone else also peered over the edge of the cliff. This man wore a National Park Service cap. He was a park ranger, she realized.

Relieved, Erin tried to suck in a few more breaths to calm herself. But the task felt impossible.

"I'm sending down the rope," the first man said. "What's your name?"

She almost didn't want to say. She didn't want the scrutiny in case any of these guys recognized her. But she had little choice right now. "I'm Erin."

"Erin, I'm Dillon. My dog, Scout, is here, too, along with four park rangers. We've already secured the end of this rope to one of our guys up here. It's not going anywhere."

As she waited for the rope to be lowered, her arm continued to lose feeling even as the pain grew. She could feel herself becoming weaker. Feel her grip slipping.

She was so afraid that some kind of natural reflex would kick in and she'd let go.

She couldn't let that happen.

As she tried to find better footing, another rock below her tumbled.

She found herself being pulled downward again.

She scrambled, using her hands and feet to find anything that might stop what was about to happen.

But there was nothing other than air to catch her.

Dillon saw the woman beginning to slip and knew he had to do something.

They hadn't come this far to lose her now.

He swung the rope down, watching as she began to slide along the rock face. Nothing was below to catch her, and that's what concerned him the most.

"Grab the rope!" he yelled.

Her feet continued to skim the surface of the rock. The movement slowed her, at least.

But if she kept going like that, she'd end up with crushed bones and a head injury, at the very least. Most likely, she wouldn't survive the impact.

As the rope dangled in front of her, her arm flailed in the air as she tried to reach for it.

"Come on..." Dillon leaned over the ledge, on his chest, and watched. He held his breath, praying she'd grasp it in time.

Just as she began to slide faster, her fingers closed over the rope and she jerked to a stop.

A moan escaped from her, seeming to be partly filled with pain and partly with relief.

But at least she was okay...for now.

"You've got to hold on to that rope," he called. "Use both hands."

"I'm doing my best." Her voice cracked. "But my arm...it hurts."

"You can do this, Erin. I know you can."

Scout barked beside him, almost as if the dog wanted to encourage her also.

She stared up at him, and something seemed to change in her gaze. Finally, she nodded. "I won't let go." She released the branch and transferred her other hand to the rope.

"I have a second rope," Dillon called. "This one has a large loop on the end. I'm going to send it down quickly. As soon as you can, I want you to pull it over your shoulders like a harness. Can you do that?"

"I'll try." Her voice sounded strained, but at least she was trying.

A moment later, the rope reached her. She did as Dillon said and wrapped it over her head and around her shoulders, pulling her arms through one at a time.

"Good girl," Dillon murmured.

If she started to slip again, at least the rope should catch her.

"Help me pull her up," Dillon said to Rick.

"I think that's… Erin Lansing," Rick muttered beside him as he grabbed the rope.

Dillon wanted to glance at his friend, but he didn't dare take his eyes off this woman. "Is that the missing girl's mom?"

"I'm nearly certain that's her."

What was she doing out here? Had she ventured down the trail looking for her daughter herself?

Dillon wanted to shake his head in dismay.

But if it had been his daughter out here—if he had a daughter—Dillon would have done the same thing. He couldn't blame the woman for that.

"Now that the rope is secure, we're going to pull you up," he called to her. "If you can, use your feet and help walk up the rock face. Grab hold of the first rope again to help you. Got it?"

"Got it." But her voice trembled as she said the words.

This would be a scary situation for any of them.

Dillon glanced at his team and nodded. They then began working together to pull her from the cliff face. Even Scout used his teeth to help pull the rope. Thankfully, the woman wasn't heavy, so the rescue should be fairly easy.

But Dillon knew this wasn't over until this woman was on solid ground.

Erin felt her body lifting as she was pulled upward. She reminded herself to keep taking deep breaths. To keep trusting these strangers.

She had no other choice at the moment.

Slowly, she rose higher and higher.

She tried to do what the man had said and use her feet to walk up the side of the cliff. She held on tightly to the rope just in case something happened.

She'd never been so terrified in her life.

Then again, that actually wasn't true.

Knowing her daughter had disappeared was entirely scarier.

Still, she was wasting valuable time here, time that the search and rescue team could be using to look for Bella.

Finally, her head rose above the side of the mountain. As it did, two men grabbed her arms and lifted her over the edge of the cliff.

The next instant, she was on her hands and knees on the path she'd been pushed off of.

On cold but solid ground. Her trembling limbs could hardly hold her up. Finally, she collapsed and rolled over.

The air rushed from her lungs as relief filled her.

She was still alive. She couldn't believe it.

The dog who'd peered over the edge of the

mountain nuzzled her. She looked up and rubbed his face, thankful for the friendly eyes. The dog was white with brown spots, had intelligent eyes, and almost looked like a small St. Bernard.

The man—Dillon—squatted beside her, concern in his brown eyes. "Are you okay?"

"I think so. Thank you. Thank you so much."

His intense expression remained focused on her. "Can you stand?"

"I think so."

He took her arm and helped her to her feet. Before he let go, Erin froze, trying to find her balance. Her head still spun from everything that had happened.

Dillon studied her face before matter-of-factly stating, "You're Bella's mom."

Erin felt her cheeks flush. "I am."

"What happened?"

"Someone pushed me."

Alarm straightened his back. "What?"

She nodded. "I was trying to cross the trail. I thought I heard someone behind me. The next thing I knew, someone shoved me and

I fell. Thankfully, I was able to catch that branch."

Dillon glanced back at the rangers, making sure they were listening. Rick nodded his affirmation.

"Did you get a glimpse of this person?"

Erin shook her head. "I didn't. I wish I had. I have no idea who would do this."

Dillon glanced at Rick again. "We'll all need to keep our eyes open just in case the person is still nearby. In the meantime, what were you even doing out here?"

"I couldn't wait any longer to search for Bella. I had to come see if I could find her myself. There's a storm coming in..."

Dillon frowned. "We need to get you to the ranger station so you can be checked out. You may have hit your head or—"

She swung her head back and forth. "No. Please. I don't want to go back to the station. I want to keep looking for my daughter."

Dillon's eyes narrowed as he continued to study her, clearly trying to measure her physical well-being and state of mind. "You're in no state to continue hiking the trail."

Her gaze latched on to his. "Please. I can do it. I can. I won't hold you back. I promise."

The man pressed his lips together in a frown before glancing at the men around him.

They all seemed to be waiting for his decision.

Erin wondered who this guy was. He didn't wear a uniform, yet he seemed to be in charge.

"I just need to find my daughter." Her voice trembled as she presented one last plea. "Please. That's all I want."

Finally, he nodded. "You can come. But don't make me regret this."

THREE

To say Dillon had reservations about letting this woman come with them would be an understatement. But if they took her back to the ranger station now, they'd be wasting too much time. Besides, the weather was turning nastier by the moment.

If Bella was out here, they needed to find her. Now.

They walked down the trail, past the narrowest section and on a path that cut through the forest. Dillon took the lead. Actually, Scout did. As Dillon walked behind him, Erin kept up the pace and remained at his side despite her rapid breaths and shaky limbs.

Erin looked younger than he'd assumed she would be, especially considering the fact she had a sixteen-year-old daughter. The woman was trim and petite with wavy dark hair that came to her chin. Her brown eyes were both perceptive and afraid. A splatter of freckles crept across her nose and cheeks.

Since the woman was with them, Dillon decided this might be a good time to get more information about the missing girl. Every detail could help.

"I'm sorry to hear about your daughter," he started, his eyes on the winding trail in front of him.

Scout tugged the lead, his nose on the scent. That was good news. There was nothing worse than a trail going cold, especially when they'd come this far. Especially when the stakes were so high.

"I just can't believe she's missing." Erin's voice sounded dull with grief. "It still seems like a nightmare that I should wake up from. But I haven't."

"Tell me what your daughter is like."

Erin drew in a deep breath. "Bella is... Where do I start? She's funny. Really funny. She makes me laugh a lot. I always think she's one of those people who could make it on a television sketch comedy one day."

"Do you like those late-night shows?" He'd never cared for them himself.

"Not really. They're not for me. But I *do* think you have to be intelligent to be funny."

"So, your daughter is smart? Is she a good student?" He tried to form a better picture in his mind.

"Not always. Bella likes socializing and…"

Dillon heard her hesitation and waited for her to continue. What was she thinking twice about before sharing?

"Bella also has anxiety," Erin finally said. "She takes medication for it every day. That's another reason why we need to find her."

He stored that information away. "What happens if she doesn't take her meds?"

Erin slowed as she climbed over an outcropping of small rocks. "Different things. Sometimes she's so anxious, she's beside herself. She can't focus or even function. Other times, she wants to avoid social situations and just be alone."

"Has she ever wandered away before?"

"No, never. That's why this is so strange to me. Plus, I got a text message."

"What did it say?"

"That I deserved this."

Dillon let that update sink in. "So you think Bella was abducted and the person who took her is mocking you?"

Tension stretched across Erin's face. "I'm not sure what to think at this point."

His mind continued to race. "Does she have a boyfriend?"

Dillon glanced at Erin as he waited for her answer. As he did, he saw her expression darken. There was another story there. He knew it.

"She likes a boy, but I told her she couldn't date yet."

"Did she give you his name?"

"No. She wouldn't tell me. But she's not mature enough to date. It was a bad idea."

"Did you tell the police that?"

"Of course. But I don't think they'll listen to anything I have to say." Her voice cracked.

Her words caught him off guard. "What do you mean?"

Erin glanced behind her at the rangers there.

"It's a long story. But my ex-husband used to be a cop."

"Is that right?" Dillon was definitely curious now. Her words alluded to a deep history—a bad history—that she'd rather put behind her.

"It wasn't a good situation," Erin continued. "And it didn't end well...to say the least."

Maybe Dillon would ask around later to find out more information. Or maybe he wouldn't. What he really wanted to concentrate on right now was finding Bella.

Scout still continued to be hot on the trail.

Dillon glanced at the sky in the distance, worried about being out here if the storm hit them. He knew just how dangerous these mountains could be. They were hard enough to hike on a good day. But add rain, wind and snow? That could be a deadly combination.

He'd give this search another hour. Then they'd need to turn back. They couldn't take the risk.

Dillon knew Erin wouldn't handle that news well.

And he couldn't blame her.

* * *

Erin fell into step behind Dillon, incredibly grateful he'd allowed her to come.

The thought of simply waiting to hear if Bella had been located made her feel like her insides were being ripped apart. Bella needed her right now—and Erin needed Bella just as much.

But Dillon's legs were long, and his dog was fast. Erin had to scramble to keep up with him and the team of rangers accompanying him. The last thing she wanted was to hold them back.

She just wanted to find her daughter. To hold her in her arms. To never let her go.

If only she could do that.

As Scout's steps slowed, Erin wedged her way closer to Dillon. He'd pointed out a set of footprints on the ground, ones that seemed to match Bella's shoe size. Based on Scout's body language, the prints followed Bella's scent.

Maybe they were onto something.

Dillon and his dog seemed competent and

exuded a sense of confidence that brought her a wave of comfort.

The man seemed like the quiet type. He had broad shoulders and serious eyes. He'd briefly taken his hat off earlier, and Erin had seen light brown hair cut close to his head. But he also seemed experienced and focused, two qualities Erin could be grateful for, especially in this situation.

His casual clothing—cargo pants, hiking boots, and a thick jacket—indicated he was a volunteer. But his command of the situation and confident actions indicated there was more to his story.

Erin needed to connect with the man. She needed him to understand how desperate she felt. She needed a team of people who wouldn't give up on finding Bella—not until she was safe at home.

However, this could all backfire if the man knew who Liam was—and if he turned out to be on Liam's side. Erin would like to think those facts wouldn't change anything, that everyone would still be helpful.

But she knew from experience that wasn't always the case.

"Beautiful dog," she murmured, glancing at the dog again. "Are you a park ranger?"

"I'm a former cop and a current search and rescue volunteer."

A former cop? Erin sucked in a breath.

It was bad enough when she thought he might simply know who Liam was. But what if he had been friends with Liam?

Even worse, what if this man was just like her abusive ex? What if he was dangerous? Or what if he was like all her ex's friends and thought Erin was guilty in Liam's disappearance?

Erin's head swam at the thoughts.

Park rangers, she could handle. Some of them might have known Liam, but that didn't necessarily mean they were on his side.

Cops? Especially local cops?

They *always* took Liam's side—even when she'd had a black eye and a bruised rib.

Erin rubbed her temples, wishing she could clear the fog from her head. She needed to be sharp if she was going to hike out here. Distraction could get her killed.

Bella's image slammed into her mind again.

She didn't want to admit it, but she wouldn't put it past Bella to run. The girl had certainly threatened to do so enough times. She'd had a rough upbringing, and the urge to run seemed to be ingrained in her.

Erin had adopted Bella from out of a bad situation six years ago. Since then, she'd showered the girl with affection, had set clear boundaries, and had even taken her to therapy multiple times a week.

But some issues were hard to fix, no matter how much love and attention someone poured onto the person in need. Still, Erin hadn't given up hope.

And she never would.

"Right here, you can see another set of footprints joins the first set." Dillon paused and pointed to an area in the dirt.

One of the rangers stepped forward to snap pictures and document the prints.

"Where did this second set come from?" Erin asked.

Dillon scanned the area around them until finally pointing to some underbrush. "Based on the direction of the shoe print, I'd say the tracks came from that direction."

Erin followed his hand as it pointed to a rocky outcropping—the perfect place for somebody to hide out and wait for someone to pass.

Dread filled Erin.

No, it was something worse than dread.

It was terror—terror at the unknown.

"What does all this mean?" Erin couldn't stop herself from asking the question, even though she already knew the answer.

Dillon offered another side-glance at her, his face remaining placid and unemotional. "That's not something I can answer. Maybe one of the rangers can tell you more."

She looked around her, noting how the other rangers seemed distracted with documenting the prints.

More memories pummeled her.

Her ex had been a good cop but a terrible husband.

A man who took his stress and anger out on Erin.

No one had believed her when she'd cried out for help. Liam had been too charming. Too convincing. Too twisted.

Now she had to live with that aftermath.

"What do *you* think it means?" She nodded down at the ground before looking back up at Dillon.

His jaw tightened as he stared at the prints. "I think it means that Bella met someone here."

"Willingly?"

"I can't answer that." He softened his voice, as if he wanted to let her know he understood but had boundaries.

Erin knew he was trying to be professional. But she needed answers, even if those answers terrified her. The truth wasn't something she could be afraid of—otherwise, she'd live her whole life in fear.

She'd done too much of that already.

She stared up at Dillon as they stood there. She wanted to keep moving. But she had to respect the rules of their investigation. She'd promised to do so before she'd headed out with them.

"You think someone abducted her, don't you?" she whispered so just Dillon could hear.

Dillon's gaze said everything even though he didn't say a word. That was *exactly* what he thought, she realized.

She buried her face in her hands—but only for a minute.

Erin couldn't fall apart. Not now.

She'd have time for that later.

Right now, all her energy needed to be focused on finding Bella. Everything else would fall in place when this was over.

Two rangers stayed behind. As they did, the rest of the group continued walking. They veered off the main trail and into the woods.

Danger seemed to hang in the air at every turn.

Just then, Scout stopped walking and sat at attention.

Erin sucked in a breath.

She knew what that meant.

It meant the K-9 had found something.

The park ranger—Rick, if Erin remembered correctly—sprang into action. Using his gloved hands, he moved away some dead leaves.

When he looked up, his expression was grim.

"We have a dead body," he announced.

Dillon pushed Erin back.

She didn't need to see the body.

Instead, he let the ranger take over the scene, and he stayed with her.

She let out a cry and nearly collapsed right there on the trail. Quickly, he reached his arm out and caught her by the elbow.

She practically sank into him as if grief consumed her until she could no longer stand up straight.

"We don't know who it is," he murmured, trying to bring her whatever reasonable comfort he could.

"Looks to me like this person has been dead for a while." Ranger Rick's voice drifted over to them as he talked to the ranger beside him.

Dillon felt Erin straighten ever so slightly.

"Is there anything else that you can tell based on what you saw?"

Dillon glanced back, trying to get a better look at the body himself.

"I would say, based on that shoe size, it's a man. Ranger Rick is right, whoever it is has been out here for a while. You can hardly make out any of his features."

"What do you mean by 'a while'?"

"It's hard to say because of the elements. The medical examiner will be better at determining that than me. But if I had to guess, I'd say maybe a year."

She let out a cry. He'd thought that would be good news, that it would bring her comfort.

"Is there something you're not telling me?" Dillon waited, more curious than ever.

She looked up at him, her eyes red-rimmed with unshed tears. "The body…is there any type of jewelry on him?"

There was *definitely* more to this.

Dillon left her for a moment and wandered toward the man for a better look. The rangers had already called backup to help them retrieve the body.

Unfortunately, this was taking time away

from their search for Bella. Part of him wanted to continue on with Scout. But it was too soon to do that.

As he studied the man, Dillon's eyes narrowed. It was hard to tell much about the body as a lot of decomposition had already started. But a piece of gold glimmered near the man's neck. He *was* wearing a piece of jewelry.

He squinted. It almost appeared to be a necklace with an eagle and a rose on it.

The jewelry was definitely unique.

"Dillon?"

He turned back toward Erin and saw the questions in her eyes.

After a moment of hesitation, he nodded. "There's a necklace."

"Does it have an eagle and a rose on it?"

His back muscles tightened at her exacting description. "It does. How did you know to ask that question?"

She ran a hand over her face, the despair on her expression making her appear years older. "Because that's the necklace my ex-husband always wore. He disappeared a year ago."

A bad feeling swelled in Dillon.

What in the world was going on here?

FOUR

Erin's thoughts continued to reel.

Could that really be Liam? Could he have been dead all this time?

Her hand went to her throat as she thought through the implications. Before, people had only *suspected* her of doing something. But now, if they had a dead body, Erin could only imagine the accusations would grow even greater.

How much more could she handle? It was a marvel that people in town hadn't yet run her off. They would have if it hadn't been for Bella.

Bella wanted to stay in Boone's Hollow to finish out high school. After that, Erin planned on finding a new place to settle down—a place away from people's watchful and accusing gazes. Somewhere where people didn't know her history and she could begin again.

"What was your ex-husband's name?"

Dillon's voice snapped Erin out of her dazed state and she turned toward him, trying to ignore the way he studied her face.

She swallowed hard before announcing, "His name was Liam. Liam Lansing."

Recognition flooded his gaze.

At that moment, Erin knew he'd no longer be on her side. At first, the former cop had seemed oblivious to her identity. It was part of the reason she'd felt drawn to him. Maybe he hadn't already formed a judgment about her.

But now all of that would be different. He'd probably look at her with the same disdain that everyone else did.

Dillon stepped closer and lowered his voice. "We don't know for sure that's him. Authorities will have to do an autopsy and get a better identification on him."

Maybe that was true, but the necklace seemed like it sealed the deal.

"What about Bella?" Erin's throat constricted as she said the words.

Liam had already taken so much away from her. But even from the grave—if that was his body—Erin wouldn't let him take away the opportunity to search for her daughter.

Dillon glanced at his phone and then up at the sky. "The storm is coming fast. We really need to head back."

"Now?" Grief—and a touch of panic—clutched her heart.

Giving up was the last thing that Erin wanted. She wanted to stay on these trails until she found her daughter.

It was only fair.

If her daughter was suffering, then Erin deserved to suffer, too. It had been her job to take care of Bella, and she'd clearly failed. Otherwise, her daughter would be safe and sound at home right now.

"What we don't want is another casualty while we're out here searching." Dillon's voice remained low and calm as he said the words, and his expression matched.

Erin tried to hold back her tears but hot

moisture pooled in her eyes. They were so close. She could feel it.

"But Scout is on the trail," she said. "We can't lose Bella's scent, and after the storm…"

Dillon pressed his lips together and Erin knew she'd made a valid point.

"We'll go a little farther," he finally said. "But it's probably going to be you, me and Scout. The rest of the team will probably want to stay here to investigate this body."

Erin nodded. She would take whatever she could get.

Dillon went and talked to Ranger Rick for several minutes before returning. A moment later, the ranger pulled out a plastic bag, opened it, and Scout sniffed the sweatshirt inside.

Bella's sweatshirt.

Scout barked before starting through the woods again.

As a brisk wind swept over the landscape, Erin shivered and was again reminded that she wasn't cut out to do this type of search and rescue mission.

But she'd do anything for her daughter.

Even if it meant getting hurt herself.

* * *

Dillon had to give Erin credit for keeping up with him. Even though she didn't look totally steady on her feet, she was making a valiant effort as they continued to traverse the rocky terrain.

But his thoughts continued to race as they moved forward.

Liam Lansing had been her husband? The fact still surprised him.

Dillon had run into the man a few times while working as a state police officer, and he'd never been impressed. Anger seemed to simmer beneath the man's gaze.

But Liam Lansing had also been the type who could be charming and attract people to him. He was the type of guy who could get people on his side.

Whether or not that body they'd found was Liam's, Dillon could only assume at this point that the man was dead. He'd been missing for at least a year. He would guess that someone Liam had put in jail had found him and exacted revenge.

Dillon paused as they came to an especially

rocky section of the trail. He reached back and helped Erin down. The last thing they needed right now was for anyone to get hurt on this trail. Planning and preparation meant they could use their time wisely.

Yet they'd already had so many setbacks.

"Thank you," Erin muttered before quickly releasing his hand.

He nodded and continued moving, not wanting to waste any more time.

Dillon knew a lot of people had blamed Liam's ex-wife for his disappearance. Looking at the woman now, seeing the fear in her eyes, he found it hard to believe that someone like Erin would be capable of something like that.

He generally had good instincts about people, and those instincts told him that Erin didn't have it inside her to hurt someone.

Still, he needed to be on guard.

A sharp wind cut through the mountain path, invading the layers of his clothing to hit his skin.

The winter storm was getting closer. Too close for comfort.

He didn't want to turn around now. Not

with Bella still missing out here and Scout still on the trail. But he was going to have to make some calls soon, calls that may not be popular with Erin.

Several minutes later, Scout reached an area where water had trickled over the trail and had now frozen.

Dillon paused.

"What's going on?" Erin asked. "What does this mean?"

"That means Scout is losing the scent," Dillon said.

"Wouldn't it make sense that the trail would continue following this path?"

"As you can see, the path goes two ways from here, one down into the valley and the other up this mountain to an overlook."

She frowned. "Which way are we going to go?"

Dillon swallowed hard before launching into his decision. "Here's the thing. We're running out of time."

Erin's eyes widened with something close to desperation. "But we're right here. We can't turn back now."

Just as she said the words, a smattering of snowflakes floated down around them. The icy precipitation brought with it the promise that more was coming.

"The weather's going to turn bad quickly," Dillon explained. "We don't want to be stuck out here when it does."

"But Bella..." Erin's voice cracked.

Dillon frowned, understanding the dilemma all too well. Understanding why she wouldn't want to leave. Understanding how heartbreaking this must feel to her.

"Erin, the truth is, we're going to be no good to Bella if we're killed out here ourselves. How would we search for her then?"

"But..." She stared at the trail in the distance, agony flashing in her gaze.

More snow began falling, snow that was mixed with freezing rain.

"Scout's lost the trail," he reminded her. "I know it seems logical that Bella went either to the left or to the right. But there are a lot of possibilities here. When the storm lets up, we'll have the helicopters out. We can put search parties out. We can narrow it down to this area. But right now, we need to get back to where it's dry and warm."

Erin said nothing.

Dillon lightly touched her arm. "I'm sorry, Erin. I know this isn't what you want to hear. But it's my job to ensure the safety of my team. Right now, you and Scout are my team."

Her hand went over her lips, almost as if she wanted to let out a cry. She didn't. Instead, she nodded resolutely. "Okay then."

Dillon studied her a moment. She seemed submissive now. But he wouldn't put it past Erin to head back out into this wilderness by herself. He needed to make sure that didn't happen.

These mountains were no place for inexperienced hikers, especially with the weather like this.

He nodded in the direction they'd just come from. "Let's get going before this turns worse. There are a few passes that will be nearly impossible if they freeze over. There's another path we can take as a shortcut to the parking lot. I think we should take that."

Erin's eyes widened as if she hadn't thought of that yet. She nodded. "Let's go. I just pray that Bella is somewhere warm and dry right now."

Erin couldn't stop thinking about everything that happened. It felt like Dillon and his team were so close to answers. With every step Scout took, his nose on the trail, she'd felt like finding Bella was within their grasp.

And then it wasn't. Just like that.

What happened to Bella's scent? How had it suddenly disappeared like that?

The whole thing didn't make any sense. Bella's scent couldn't have just disappeared out of the blue, right?

Erin's heart pounded harder, louder, into her ears as anxiety squeezed her again.

All she wanted was her daughter safe and in her arms.

Out of the unknown. Out of these harsh elements.

The wind was so, so cold, and turning cooler by the moment. What if Bella didn't have shelter?

At that thought, Erin decided she'd come back here herself if she had to—at the first chance she had.

Erin started forward when Dillon pointed to another trail cutting through the forest.

"This is going to be a shortcut back to the parking lot," he said. "I think we need to go this way."

Disappointment filled her. She'd hoped to again go past the scene where they'd found that body, before taking the shortcut. She'd hoped to hear if the rangers had any updates for her.

But it didn't look like that was an option right now.

Instead, she nodded and continued walking.

Several minutes later, Dillon nodded toward a rocky ledge they would have to cross ahead. "We're going to need to be very careful at this section."

Even from where Erin stood, she could already see that the trail was slick. There was no handrail. Just a sheer drop—one similar to the area where Erin had been pushed.

Her heart raced as she remembered her earlier fall. As she remembered the person who had done that to her.

"Can you tell me more about what happened before you felt someone push you off that cliff?" Dillon asked.

Erin shrugged, wishing she didn't have to replay the scene. But she knew it was necessary if they were going to find answers. "I thought I heard somebody in the woods behind me a couple of times. Then I thought maybe I was imagining things. I wasn't really sure. But the next thing I knew, I felt two hands on my back and I began falling."

"Who would have done that?" He glanced back at her.

"The person who grabbed Bella?"

"Why would the person who took her follow you and try to kill you?" Dillon's eyes looked just as intelligent as Scout's as the man observed her, his thoughts clearly racing as he tried to put the pieces together.

She shook her head. "I wish I knew."

Erin sucked in a breath as she began to walk along the rocky ledge. Panic wanted to seize her.

She'd wanted to argue with the decision to turn back, but Dillon had been right to make the call. If they had been trapped out in a snowstorm, all three of them would also be in danger. As much as she hated to leave, staying out here wasn't an option.

"Keep your steps steady and slow. You can do this."

Dillon's words sounded surprisingly comforting, and Erin was grateful he was there with her.

She did as he said and moved carefully. As she started to look down, she paused. She glimpsed the vast expanse below her and quickly averted her gaze.

She couldn't put herself in that mindset. She just needed to focus on where she was going, not where she *could* go if she slipped up.

That was what she always used to tell Bella also. *You have to focus on the road ahead while remembering the lessons behind you.*

Erin's heart panged with grief as she thought about her daughter again.

Often, she'd wished she could go back to the sweet times when Bella had only been ten or eleven. Times when they'd had fun going on road trips. When they'd cooked together. When Erin had braided Bella's hair and they'd painted each other's fingernails.

But something had happened as soon as the girl turned fifteen. It was almost like her daughter had transformed into a different person. Certainly, hormones had played a role in that. But so had Liam. That had been when Liam's anger problems had worsened. When he'd stopped trying to hide from Bella that he took his frustrations out on Erin.

That's when Erin had known she'd had to get out. Not only had the relationship become unhealthy for her, it had also become unhealthy for Bella.

Finally, Erin stepped onto solid ground again. She breathed a sigh of relief once she was finished with the crossing.

As she did, she glanced back and saw Dillon and Scout carefully walking past the area. They did it with much more grace and ease than she had.

They continued walking. Erin wished she could carry on a conversation as they did so, but the air had turned colder and hurt her lungs. She pulled her coat higher and tried to breathe into the collar.

But as the snow came down harder, her discomfort grew. She had to watch every step. Concentrate every thought on getting out of this forest in one piece and without any broken bones.

Finally, they reached the clearing where the parking lot was.

When she walked over to her car, she pulled in a deep breath.

Her tires had been slashed.

Tears pressed her eyes as she soaked in the deep gashes in the rubber.

Who would have done this?

As Dillon stared at the slashed tires on Erin's car, a bad feeling began to grow inside him. Somebody was bent on making Erin suffer.

Why was that? And who would want to do something like this?

"I'm going to send a crew out to look at

your tires," he told her. "But right now, we need to get out of the elements."

"Of course." Erin continued to stare at her vehicle as she said the words, but her eyes looked duller now than they had earlier.

"I'm parked over here." Dillon nodded to his Jeep. "How about I give you a ride? Would you be okay with that?"

She stared at him a moment as if contemplating her answer before finally nodding. "I would appreciate that. Thank you."

"It's no problem."

They walked across the parking lot to his Jeep. He helped Erin into the front seat before lifting Scout into the back. Then Dillon climbed in and cranked the engine. As he waited for the vehicle to heat, he gave Scout some water. Then he reached into the back and grabbed a blanket.

He'd just washed it, and the scent of fabric softener still smelled fresh between the folds. He handed it to Erin. "This will help take the edge off until the heat kicks in."

"Thank you." Her teeth practically chattered as she said the words.

As the air slowly warmed and heat poured from the vents, it offered a welcome relief from the otherwise frigid temperatures outside.

"I'm going to go ahead and call about your tires now before we take off," Dillon explained. "I'd also like to see if there are any updates on our search mission, as well as the dead body."

"Of course." She pulled the blanket higher around her shoulders.

He dialed Rick's number and his friend answered on the first ring. Dillon explained that they'd come back from the hike and told Rick about Erin's tires being slashed.

"How about you?" Dillon asked. "Any updates?"

"We were able to retrieve the body before the snowstorm came. I'll take it back to the medical examiner's office to get some more answers. We also recorded the scene and tried to find any evidence that had been left behind there."

"Hopefully, you'll get some answers to that soon."

"I'm glad you called," Rick said. "Chief Blackstone called and wants to know if you can bring Erin in for some additional questions."

Chief Blackstone? Dillon didn't know the man well, but he'd worked with the Boone's Hollow police chief on a couple of operations. He'd found the man to be overbearing and quick-tempered. In other words, he wasn't Dillon's favorite person.

Dillon glanced at Erin, aware that she had no idea what they were talking about. Instead, she reached back and rubbed Scout's head.

Dillon looked away, turning his attention back to the situation. "I'm sure I can do that. Do you know what it's pertaining to?"

"I think he has more questions for her concerning Bella's disappearance. That's all that they told me."

"Very well." Dillon ended the call and glanced at Erin again, wondering how she was going to take this update.

He cleared his throat before saying, "The chief would like to speak with you."

Her face seemed to go a little paler. "Why?"

"I'm sure it's just routine."

She squeezed her lips together before saying, "Nothing is routine when it comes to Chief Blackstone. The man hates me."

Dillon wanted to refute her statement. But he couldn't.

He didn't know what exactly she'd been through after Liam, and it wouldn't be fair to state an opinion based only on a guess.

"I can stay with you and give you a ride home afterward," he offered.

The breath seemed to leave her lungs for a moment and she stared at him as if trying to read his intention. "You would do that? I'm sure you need to get home and tend to your dog."

"I don't mind."

Maybe it was curiosity or maybe it was concern. But Dillon wanted to stay with Erin and find out exactly what was going on here. Plus, he sensed that this woman didn't really have anyone else to help her.

Giving her a ride was the least that he could do.

He put his Jeep into Reverse and backed

out. "Let's get going. The storm isn't going to be letting up anytime soon, and these roads can get bad."

Erin nodded and crossed her arms over her chest.

She had to be living a nightmare right now. Dillon just prayed that she would have a happy ending.

FIVE

Erin knew Dillon was trying to paint this visit to the police station in a positive light for her sake. But she knew the truth.

She knew how this would play out.

Just as when Liam had disappeared, Erin was most likely going to be the main suspect in Bella's disappearance as well.

Didn't Blackstone and his crew know that she would never hurt her daughter? These guys just needed a suspect and, for some reason, Erin seemed to fit the bill.

A sickly feeling began to grow in her stomach. She didn't want to go to the police station. But if she ran, she'd only look guilty. On the other hand, if she were arrested, how could she help find her daughter?

The questions collided inside her until Erin felt off-balance.

What was she going to do? What if Blackstone *did* try to arrest her?

And was Dillon just playing nice? Was he playing good cop trying to get information from her?

Erin wished she could trust men in uniform. Most of them were probably good guys. But the ones she knew weren't. Their loyalties were misplaced and their justice biased.

She stared at the road in front of her. To say the weather had become blustery would be an understatement. It was downright nasty out here.

In fact, it was nearly impossible to even see the road as the snow created whiteout conditions.

She uncrossed her arms and grabbed the armrest, trying to remain calm.

She remembered the time in her life back before she'd met Liam. She'd been so carefree and happy. As an only child whose parents had been divorced, she'd been determined to make a different future for herself.

But everything had changed and she could hardly remember that idealistic person anymore. Her parents had both remarried and started new lives. She hardly ever spoke to them anymore.

"This could get slippery," Dillon muttered.

As far as she was concerned, slippery roads and mountains didn't mix. "Are you good at driving in snow?"

"I'd like to think so. This girl hasn't let me down yet." He patted the dash of his Jeep.

Erin glanced into the back seat and saw that Scout looked pretty laidback as well. Couldn't dogs sense danger? Maybe the fact that Scout looked relaxed was a good sign. Maybe the dog knew things Erin didn't.

The road turned with the bends in the mountain. Erin had come up this way a few times before, and she knew that at one point the road traveled alongside the path of a stream. Then it climbed back up the mountain. Eventually, it even became a gravel road.

The truth was that, even on a good day, the road was hard to manage. Throw in this kind of weather and the trip was even scarier.

Erin pressed her eyes shut.

Dear Lord, I know You haven't let me down

yet. Please, be with me now. Everything is falling apart, and I feel helpless. But I know I have You. I know You have a plan. I just need You now more than ever.

She'd prayed prayers like that before, especially when she'd been with Liam. It was so easy to think that things couldn't get worse.

But life had proven to her that they could, indeed, get worse.

Would that be the case now also?

Erin glanced outside again, trying to get a glimpse of where they were. Dillon was traveling slowly, which made her feel better, more secure.

But she sensed something shift in the air. It was Dillon's body language, she realized. He seemed more tense. More alert. Had something happened?

She glanced behind her, desperate for answers. "Dillon?"

He gripped the steering wheel and glanced into the rearview mirror again. "I think we're being followed."

"You mean somebody is just behind us?"

Even as she said the words, she knew they didn't sound correct.

His jaw tightened. "I can't be sure. Most people in their right mind aren't out on the road right now."

The breath left her lungs.

Erin knew what he was getting at. There hadn't been anybody behind them in the parking lot when they'd left. The rescue crew and the remaining rangers had already left. Only Erin's car had remained behind. Not only that, but there were no other roads between that lot and where they were on the road now.

That meant somebody had parked on the side of the street.

Had that person waited for Dillon and Erin to go past and then pulled out behind them?

She remembered the person who'd pushed her down the cliff. What if that person was following them now? What if that person wanted to fix the mistake they'd made earlier when Erin hadn't died?

Dillon hadn't wanted to alarm Erin. But the woman was observant and had noticed the tension threading through him. It was only fair of him to tell her the truth.

Right now, the car behind him maintained a steady distance. Dillon could barely see the vehicle. Occasionally, he got a glimpse between the drifts of snow coming down.

The drive was already treacherous. The last thing he needed was somebody tailing them. Dillon just hoped that the person behind them would maintain a steady pace and not try to do anything foolish.

He quickly glanced at Erin and saw that she seemed to be getting paler and paler. If somebody was following them, was this person connected to Bella's disappearance? Could it be the same person who'd pushed Erin off the cliff?

If Erin were guilty in her daughter's disappearance, why would somebody be going through all this trouble?

Dillon knew the answer to that question. They wouldn't.

So many questions collided in his head, but this wasn't the time to think about them.

Right now, he needed to focus all his attention on the road.

He gently pressed on the brake as the road in front of him disappeared into a blur of white. He looked for any type of markers to show him where he needed to be.

There were too many unknowns in this area. Even though Dillon had driven this path many times, he hadn't memorized every inch of it. He hadn't remembered every turn and every drop-off. The lane was already narrow.

In different circumstances, he might pull off and try to wait the storm out. But the snow showers weren't supposed to be over until tomorrow. Forecasters hadn't even known that this system was going to come on this quickly, either.

Pulling off right now could be deadly. Especially if somebody else heading down the road wasn't expecting him to be there. Visibility was nearly down to zero.

Dillon glanced in his rearview mirror again and saw a brief glimpse of the car.

His heart rate quickened.

The vehicle was closer, probably only six feet behind them.

Was that on purpose? Dillon didn't know. But his gut told him he needed to remain on guard.

"Dillon?" Erin's voice sounded shaky beside him.

"Yes?"

"What's going on?" She still gripped the armrest.

"I'm just taking this moment by moment." He didn't bother to hide the truth.

"I don't even know how you're driving in this. It's completely white all around us."

"That's why I'm going slow. My Jeep has excellent traction." Those things were the truth. But there were many other hazards he didn't mention.

Just as the words left his mouth, he felt something nudge the car.

It was the vehicle behind them.

The driver was trying to run them off the road, wasn't he?

Dillon had to think quick if he wanted to

walk away from this drive with his life—and the lives of those in his vehicle—intact.

As Erin felt the Jeep lurch forward, a muffled scream escaped.

Somebody *had* been following them.

And now somebody wanted to run them off the road.

Her thoughts swirled.

This couldn't really be happening...but it was.

She glanced behind her and could barely make out headlights there. From what she could tell, this guy was gearing up to ram them again.

Next time, she and Dillon may not be so lucky. That driver might succeed and push them right off one of these cliffs.

It was nearly impossible to see what was about to happen. Erin had no idea if the Jeep was at the center of the road, if anybody was coming toward them, or how close they were to the cliff on one side of them or the river on the other.

She squeezed her eyes shut and began to pray even more fervently.

Dillon could be as experienced a driver as there was out there, but his skills would only get them so far in these circumstances.

Please, protect us. Guide us. I can't die. Not with Bella still out there. Please.

Scout let out a whine in the back seat. Erin reached back and rubbed his head, feeling his soft fur beneath her hand. "It's going to be okay, boy."

Comforting the dog helped distract her from her own fear.

The reprieve didn't last long.

The vehicle behind them rammed them again. This time, the Jeep careened out of control.

Erin gasped as they slid down the mountain road. The tires hit rocks and began to bump, bump, bump over them.

She squeezed her eyes shut as the bottom dropped from her stomach.

Where would they stop?

She didn't know. But she prepared herself to hit water. To hit a rock wall. To soar from a cliff.

To die.

SIX

"Hold on!" Dillon yelled.

Dillon fought to maintain control of the vehicle. But it was no use.

The icy road was winning.

Now he just had to work with the situation.

As he jerked the wheel, trying to avoid going off an unseen cliff, Erin gasped beside him.

The other vehicle revved its engine as it sped past them.

He strained to get a glimpse of who might be behind the wheel or what the vehicle looked like.

It was no use. All he'd seen was a flash of gray.

Finally, the Jeep slid to a stop.

Dillon let out a breath, halfway still expecting the worst. A sudden fall from the cliff or for the ground to disappear from beneath them.

But nothing happened.

His heart pounded in his ears as they sat there for a moment.

Then he glanced at Erin. "Are you okay?"

She let out a long, shaky breath. "I think so. You?"

He nodded. "That was close, to say the least. Did you get a glimpse of the vehicle when it went past?"

She shook her head, appearing disappointed she didn't have more to share. "All I saw was that it seemed to be gray. But everything... the snow was so thick that it was almost impossible and—"

"I know. You don't have to explain." He reached into the back seat and rubbed Scout.

The dog appeared to be okay still. They were *all* okay. That was good news.

But what waited for them next?

Dillon let out a long breath.

The three of them couldn't stay here. It was dangerous for any oncoming traffic, for starters. Plus, Dillon had no idea exactly where they were.

Had they skidded onto a pull-off on the side of the road? Had they hit a rocky patch of the road itself? He wasn't sure.

Based on the fact that he'd seen the car zoom past them on the right side, he could assume the roadway was there.

What would happen when Dillon started traveling down the road again? Was the other driver going to wait for them to pass and try these shenanigans again?

He wanted to say no. But he really had no idea.

"Should we call for backup?" Erin's voice cracked with fear.

He grabbed his phone and looked at the screen. It was just as he thought. There was no signal out here. Most places in these mountains didn't have a signal.

He frowned. "We're going to have to see if we can make it out of here ourselves. It's the best option of what we've got."

Erin rubbed her throat as if she were having

trouble swallowing, but she nodded. "Whatever you think is best."

Dillon wished he knew what was best. There had been a time when he'd trusted his instincts. When his life had depended on doing so.

But after what had happened with Masterson, that was no longer the case.

He let out a long breath before slowly pulling onto what he hoped was the road. He waited for a moment, hoping for a break in the snow or the wind—something just enough to allow him to see where he was.

A moment later, he got his wish. The snow seemed to hold its breath and offered him a glimpse of the winter wonderland around them.

Dillon could barely make out a street sign in the distance—but it was something. That was where he needed to head.

At this rate, it would take him at least an hour to get to the Boone's Hollow police station, if not more.

He didn't care about how long it took, only that they arrived safe.

He began inching back down the road, ignoring the ache that had formed between his shoulder blades.

This wasn't the kind of weather people needed to be out driving in. Back when he'd been a cop, he'd seen way too many accidents happen in conditions like these. He didn't want to be one of those statistics.

Still, he pressed forward.

The good news was that the other car hadn't appeared again.

Maybe the driver had assumed they'd crashed. That would be the best-case scenario for them now.

Once they managed to get through this crisis, Dillon knew there would be another one waiting for them at the police station.

He never thought his day would turn into this.

He glanced over at Erin.

He was certain that she hadn't thought that, either.

Erin's relief was short-lived.

They'd finally managed to get off the mountain backroad and onto a highway. But now they'd pulled up to the police station. Now she was going to be facing another type of struggle.

You could run, a quiet voice said inside her.

She reminded herself again that, if she ran, she'd only look guilty. Besides, she had nothing to hide, nothing to be ashamed of.

As soon as Dillon parked the Jeep, she glanced over at him.

Something shifted in him also, almost as if arriving at the station had caused him to shift personas. Or was that only what Liam did?

Her emotions tangled with her logic until nothing made sense.

Was he getting ready to treat her like she was a criminal? Had he secretly needed to bring her in for questioning?

Erin didn't know the man well enough to say so. She only knew he was handsome and kind and brave. Not that any of those things mattered right now. There were so many more important things to worry about.

"Thanks for getting us off that mountain," she finally said instead.

Dillon nodded, his gaze still assessing hers. "It's no problem. I'm glad we're all okay right now. It was a close call back there."

That was an understatement. Erin's life had flashed before her eyes again—for the second time in one day.

He nodded toward the modest, one-story building in the distance. "Are you ready to head inside?"

She stared at the police building. It was still snowing, but at this very moment, it wasn't coming down hard. Memories flooded back to her.

Memories of bringing Liam lunch while he was on his break. Of the hope she'd felt when he'd first gotten the job.

Then she remembered how hostile it had all become when things went south. The uneasy feeling she'd felt whenever she'd stepped inside.

Was she ready to relive those moments? Not really.

That's why she'd gone to the park rangers when Bella went missing, instead of the local police. But she'd known they would eventually get involved.

She didn't need to tell Dillon all that. He'd already carried enough of her burdens today.

She'd never answered his question. *Are you ready to go inside?*

"I suppose I'm ready," she finally said, wishing her heart wasn't beating so hard and fast.

Dillon stared at her another moment, something unspoken in his gaze. Erin wished she knew what he was thinking, but she didn't know him well enough to ask. Besides, he didn't owe her anything—definitely not an explanation.

"Let's go." He opened his door and a brisk wind swept inside.

Moving quickly, he retrieved Scout from the back seat. As he did, Erin climbed out and pulled her jacket closer as she ambled to the front doors of the station. The lot was slippery and snow still seemed to stockpile on the ground. The sudden darkness wasn't helping, either.

This place had so many bad memories. At

one time, the building had seemed like a place of hope. When Liam first got his job here, it was like a dream come true for him. They'd even gone out to his favorite restaurant to celebrate afterward.

But Erin had never envisioned the ways that Liam would change. Not only had his personality shifted, so had the way he'd treated her. She wasn't sure what exactly had caused that change in him, but Erin had borne the brunt of his frustrations.

She continued to carefully plod over the icy surface, headed toward the front door of the building with Dillon by her side.

It certainly hadn't helped that Liam was a likable guy. He was the type of person who could make friends wherever he went. In fact, he would have made a great salesman.

Erin couldn't be certain about everything Liam must have said about her at work. But it was clear he hadn't painted her in a positive light around his colleagues.

That was why, when he disappeared, Erin was one of the first people they'd looked at.

The betrayal still hurt. At one time, these

people had been her friends. In the blink of an eye, they'd turned against her. Sometimes, it felt like everyone in town had turned against her.

As she hurried toward the front door, Dillon lightly placed his hand on her back. His concern—or was it his touch?—caused her breath to catch.

His concern. It was definitely his concern that had caused that reaction.

It had been a long time since anyone had wanted to be associated with her. For someone like Dillon to go out of his way to offer a small measure of comfort and assistance touched her in surprising ways.

They reached the front door and Dillon opened it for her. Erin slipped into the warmth of the police building.

But the welcome of warmth was short-lived. As soon as she saw Chief Blackstone head toward her, a deep chill wracked her body.

The look in his eyes indicated that her troubles were just starting.

And, unfortunately, she already felt like she was at her breaking point.

* * *

Dillon watched as Chief Blackstone's eyes instantly darkened as soon as he saw Erin.

The man was in his early forties, with only a fringe of dark hair around the sides of his rectangular head. His burly frame and stiff movements made him an intimidating figure—for some people, at least.

The man obviously had a chip on his shoulder for the woman. Dillon's curiosity spiked. Just what had transpired after Liam disappeared?

"Erin, I'd like to see you in my office." Blackstone's voice didn't contain even an ounce of warmth.

She nodded, looking resigned to that fact and like a lamb going in for the slaughter.

"Dillon, I'd like to talk with you also," Blackstone called. "Can you wait around?"

Dillon glanced at Erin, wishing he could go with her and shield her from some of what was about to happen. Because, based on the look in Blackstone's eyes, he was about to give her the third degree. Most likely, he'd show no mercy.

Why did he feel such a protective instinct toward the woman? It didn't make sense.

But he could feel the heartache she was going through right now. Plus, based on what had happened today and what he'd experienced with her, Dillon didn't believe she'd had any part in her daughter's disappearance. It just didn't make sense. She had no motive for harming her daughter.

Dillon planted himself near the door, still gripping Scout's lead. "I'll stick around."

Blackstone nodded to him.

Erin gave him one last glance before following the chief into his office.

Chief Blackstone cast a glance at Dillon before closing his door. Dillon clutched Scout's lead as he wondered exactly what was about to go down.

He hesitated a moment, unsure what to do with himself.

As he thought about everything Erin had already been through—about the grief in her gaze—something stirred inside him.

The woman had no one to stand up for her. No one to lean on.

That just wasn't right.

If Dillon's instincts were correct, she was about to experience another nightmare in the chief's office.

He couldn't let that happen.

As instinct took over, he started toward the chief's door. He knocked but pushed it open before Blackstone could answer.

"Yes?" A shadow crossed the chief's gaze.

"I'm wondering if I could stay in here and assist you with anything that you need to talk about."

Chief Blackstone narrowed his eyes. "Why would you want to do that?"

"I've been with Erin all day, so I can offer my perspective on today's events also. Including the fact that we were almost run off the road and her tires were slashed."

The chief stared at him a moment until finally nodding. "I suppose that's fine. As long as it's also fine with Erin."

Erin glanced at him and something that looked like relief flooded her face. "Yes, that's fine."

He stepped inside and closed the door. He and Scout stood in the corner, out of the way.

"Where were you when Bella disappeared?" The chief didn't waste any time before jumping right in and focusing his accusation on Erin.

Erin quickly shook her head as if the question had startled her. "Where was I? I was at work. I have a whole classroom full of kids who can verify that."

He glowered. "But what about before that?"

"Before I went to school?" She blinked several times as if his question didn't make sense. "I was getting ready to go to school, just like I do every day."

"And nobody was with you?"

She shook her head, and Dillon sensed her rising frustration.

"As I'm sure you know, the elementary school starts before the high school," Erin said. "So I left the house by seven that morning to head into school. Bella was in the bathroom getting ready when I left and that was the last time I saw her. I went through this with the park rangers."

The chief's expression showed no reaction—except maybe a tinge of skepticism. "You haven't talked to Bella since then?"

"That's correct. I've tried her cell, but she hasn't answered. I've texted her. Nothing."

"And your car was found parked beside the trailhead also…"

Erin's lips parted as if the chief's questions continued to shock her. "My car was only there because I drove to the area to search for her myself."

"Somebody said your car was there yesterday right after school hours."

Erin sucked in a breath, her eyes widening with outrage. "That's a lie. I didn't go there yesterday. I didn't even know that Bella's car had been found there until this morning. Who told you that?"

"It doesn't matter. I'm just telling you what a witness has come forward to say."

She swung her head back and forth in adamant denial. "Then somebody is trying to set me up. Are there security cameras there at the lot?"

Chief Blackstone shook his head. "I'm afraid there aren't."

"Well, you can talk to my neighbors. They'll tell you that I came home after school. That's when I realized that Bella wasn't there and I started making phone calls."

"I'd say that's a problem. We talked to your neighbors and none of them said they saw you."

"What?" Her voice trailed off.

Dillon felt a stab of outrage burst through him. "Are you accusing Erin of her daughter's disappearance?"

Blackstone's raised eyebrows showed annoyance at the question. "We're trying to cover all our bases here."

"Well, I can personally attest to the fact that her tires were slashed and someone tried to run us off the road. That's not to mention the fact that Erin was pushed off a cliff. If she was truly guilty, why did all those things happen?"

"That's a good question." The chief practically smirked. "One we need to look into."

Dillon's back muscles tightened. The chief obviously had a target on Erin's back.

If Blackstone was already convinced he knew what had happened, he wouldn't look at anyone else except Erin.

That didn't make things look promising as far as finding Bella.

SEVEN

Erin looked up and tried to offer Dillon a grateful smile.

She was glad he was there, even though she still wasn't sure why he'd barged into the chief's office. Still, his presence brought with it a strange comfort.

At first, she'd feared Dillon was one of the chief's minions. But the protective set of his jaw made her believe otherwise.

She hoped she wasn't wrong; that Dillon wasn't some kind of spy for the law enforcement head. Blackstone had so many people in his pocket that it made it hard for Erin to know whom to trust.

"Is there any other reason why you want to keep Ms. Lansing here?" Dillon's gaze locked with the chief's.

Chief Blackstone's eyes hardened. "We just wanted to hear her version of events again."

"I told you. So now, you tell me. Do you have any leads on Bella?" Erin rushed to ask, trying to keep the exasperation from her voice. But it was hard to do that when she felt like they were wasting valuable time. "Have you heard anything else? I'm so worried about her."

"No. Nothing yet." Chief Blackstone's expression—and tone—showed no emotion or regret.

Disappointment cut deep inside her. Erin had hoped for something more, even though she'd fully expected him to say those words. Once a person was guilty of something in this man's eyes, then they were always guilty. Always a suspect. Never to be trusted.

"Unless there's something else you need, I need to get her home." Dillon gripped her arm, nearly pulling Erin from her seat. "The weather is turning bad."

Erin's breath caught. Would this work? Would Dillon actually be able to get her out of here?

Chief Blackstone raised his eyebrows, a shadow darkening his glare. "*You* do? Is that right?"

Dillon shrugged. "Like I said, her tires were slashed."

Scout barked as if adding his agreement.

The chief nodded slowly, unspoken judgment lingering in his gaze. "I can get one of my guys to give her a ride home."

"That won't be necessary," Dillon said. "I don't mind."

Erin held her breath as she waited for the chief's response. Scout sat at attention as if he was also waiting.

Chief Blackstone's eyebrows flickered before he tilted his head in a nod. "Very well then. We'll be in touch if we have any more questions."

Erin wished the chief had said they'd be in touch if they had any more updates. But the way he'd worded the statement made it clear he still thought Erin could be guilty.

How could the chief think that? Did he hate her that much?

Right now, Erin just wanted to get out of there.

She stood and headed toward the door before the chief could ask anything else.

Without another word, Dillon directed her outside.

As she stepped into the lot, she noted that snow was still coming down but not as heavily as earlier. Still, the ground was covered with the icy, white flakes. The ride home would be slippery.

"Hello, Erin," someone said behind her.

She turned and saw Officer Brad Hollins standing there.

A friendly face.

He'd been a rookie who'd trained under Liam. The man had eaten at their house and come to cookouts. He was one of the few people who hadn't turned his back on Erin when everything went down.

"Hi, Officer Hollins." She paused. "You're looking good."

He grinned, but it quickly faded. "I'm sorry to hear about Bella. I'm keeping my eyes and ears open for any leads. I just wanted to let you know that."

"I appreciate it. Thank you."

She said goodbye before continuing to the Jeep. They all climbed inside. Only when the engine started did Dillon speak.

"Old friend?" he asked.

"He's one of the good guys. He's always been kind to me."

"Good. I'm glad to hear that. Listen, I'm sorry about that back there." Compassion wound through the strands of Dillon's voice.

Erin swallowed hard and glanced at her hands as they rested in her lap. What did she even say? If she overshared, would that make Dillon suspicious of her?

She finally settled on the obvious. "In case you can't tell, the chief doesn't really like me."

"Because of Liam?"

She nodded as she remembered the comradery the two men had shared. "Blackstone thought of Liam as a son."

"I see. So, Blackstone took it hard when Liam disappeared?"

"He did. He had tunnel vision and thought I was responsible for it. He was so convinced it was me, he hardly looked at any other possibility."

Dillon frowned. "I can see him doing that..."

She turned toward him and studied his face, his expression, for any sign that he was on Blackstone's side. "You mean you didn't fall under the chief's spell? Under Liam's spell?"

"I try, to the best of my ability, not to fall under spells." He offered a small grin.

Erin wanted to smile in return but she didn't. This was no time to find any kind of enjoyment out of her circumstances.

"Now, where do I need to take you?" Dillon asked.

She rattled off her address, which was located about ten minutes from the police station, just on the outskirts of town.

Using the same caution on the slippery streets as earlier, Dillon started down the road toward her place.

As the station disappeared from sight, at once she felt every ounce of her exhaustion.

What a day.

She needed to get a good night's rest so she could start again tomorrow. If it wasn't for the weather, she would keep searching tonight. But it would do no good, and she knew that.

"How long have you lived here?" Dillon's voice cut through the silence.

"I moved to Boone's Hollow when Liam and I got married, and he got a job on the force."

"Is that right? But Liam was a local, wasn't he?"

She nodded, surprised that he knew as much about Liam as he did. Then again, maybe she shouldn't be surprised. "He was. Born and raised in Boone's Hollow."

"I see. Where did you meet him? If you don't mind me asking..."

Her mind drifted back in time. "In college. Liam was studying criminal justice and I was working on my teaching degree."

"Do you teach at a local school?"

Erin shook her head. "I work two towns over. I switched after Liam went missing. It's a forty-minute drive both ways, but I figure it's worth it just for the peace of mind."

His jaw tightened. "I can't even imagine what that must be like. I'm surprised you haven't moved."

"I thought about it many times. And it's

tempting. But Bella wants to graduate from high school here. Thankfully, she hasn't gotten as bad of a rap as I did. People still seem to like her because she's Liam's daughter." She frowned as she said the words.

It was a wonder they'd accepted Bella as much as they had, especially considering that Liam wasn't her biological dad.

The thoughts continued to turn over in Erin's head.

Finally, they turned onto the street she lived off of. It wasn't in a neighborhood but instead her home was a smaller cabin located on a back road. The woods surrounding the property offered her some privacy, which had been welcome the week that everything had happened.

But as Dillon pulled up to her house and his headlights shone on the front of it, she saw a message that had been spray-painted there.

It was the word "Killer."

The blood drained from her face.

Somebody had wanted to send a message, and it had worked.

* * *

As Dillon stared at the word painted on the front of Erin's house, the severity of the situation hit him once again.

Not only was this woman's daughter missing, but people in this town were bent on making it seem like Erin was responsible. He could only imagine the pressure Erin felt right now.

As Dillon glanced at her, he saw the tears well in her eyes as she stared at the painted letters on her porch. What a shock it must be for her to see this.

"Let me make sure you get inside okay," he said.

She quickly wiped her eyes before waving her hands in the air. "You don't have to do that. You've already gone above and beyond."

"I'd feel better if I was able to check it out for you. I can't leave you here now when danger could be lurking just out of sight. I wouldn't be able to live with myself if something happened to you."

After another quick moment of hesitation, she finally nodded. "Okay then."

He took his key out of the ignition before climbing out and grabbing Scout from the back seat. Cautiously, he walked toward the front of the house, scanning everything around them as he did so.

He didn't see anybody waiting out of sight. But they still needed to be cautious.

"Stay behind me," he muttered as Erin trailed close to him.

He looked again at the letters across the front of her house. They'd been scrawled in red spray paint—of course. The color only added to the threatening effect.

How could someone do this? How could they think Erin was guilty without even knowing any details?

His stomach clenched at the thought of it.

The keys rattled in Erin's hand until finally she managed to open the door.

"Let me. Wait here." Dillon pushed himself in front of her and motioned for her to stay in the living room near the door while he checked out the rest of the place. He handed her Scout's leash, and Erin grasped it as if it were a lifeline.

Dillon checked out the house, but everything appeared clear. No threatening messages. Lurking intruders. Unsightly surprises.

As he met Erin in the living room, a fresh round of hesitancy filled him. He didn't want to leave her. She looked terrified with her wide eyes, shallow breaths and death grip on Scout's leash.

He wished he knew her better. Wished he was pushier.

But that wasn't his place. Not right now. Not when considering he'd only known her for less than twenty-four hours.

"Should I call the police?" Erin remained plastered against the wall, almost as if she were frozen in place.

Dillon let out a long breath as he considered her question. In ordinary circumstances, he would definitely say yes. But he'd seen the way the chief had spoken to Erin. Most likely, if she called for help, they wouldn't take her request seriously. Not only that, but no evidence as to who had done this had been left behind.

"How about this?" Dillon started. "I'll take a picture of the message that was left so we can record it as evidence. Then I'm going to clean it off."

"You don't have to do—"

"I want to." His voice remained firm, leaving no room for questions. "If you want to do something, how about you fix some coffee and maybe light a fire? After I finish cleaning this up, I'm going to need to warm up."

Erin stared at him another moment, hesitation in her gaze. Finally, she nodded. "Okay. If you don't mind, that would be a huge help."

She gathered the supplies he needed. Then Dillon went outside and did exactly as he'd promised. Scout stayed inside with Erin. She'd put some water in a bowl for him, and Dillon had pulled the canine's food from his backpack.

He knew Erin was in good hands with Scout. Not only was the dog an expert in search and rescue operations, Scout was also protective.

As Dillon scrubbed the spray paint, his mind went back to his own guilt. The accusations others had flung at him.

He knew what it was like to be guilty in the eyes of those around you. He knew what the weight of those accusations felt like. Maybe that's why he felt so compassionate toward Erin now. In some ways, he felt like he could understand.

As soon as Dillon finished washing the paint off, he stepped inside. The scent of fresh-brewed coffee filled his senses.

Erin waited for him to take his coat off before handing him a steaming mug.

"Smell's great. Thank you."

"I made a few sandwiches, too, just in case you're hungry." She nodded toward a tray she'd put together on the kitchen counter.

"That was thoughtful. Thank you." Now that she'd mentioned it, he was hungry. He hadn't eaten much all day.

He'd drink his coffee, eat a sandwich, and warm up a few minutes before heading back to his place.

But he doubted he'd get any sleep tonight as he wondered how Erin was doing…and if she was safe.

Erin was so grateful for Dillon. He'd truly been a godsend. If he hadn't been there for her today, she might not be alive right now.

Her throat tightened at the thought.

As she sat in a chair near the fireplace, her hands trembled. She attempted to take another sip of her coffee, but everything was tasteless. Enjoying herself was a luxury she didn't deserve right now, especially not when she thought about Bella.

Bella...

Erin continued to pray that God would protect the girl right now, whatever she was going through—whether Bella had been abducted or if she were wandering lost in the woods. Whatever the case, Erin only wanted her daughter to be safe.

However, she remembered that second set of footprints.

It looked like someone had abducted her daughter, just as she'd feared.

The hollow pit in her stomach filled with nausea at the thought of it.

"Tell me about Bella." Dillon leaned forward in his chair, his eyes fixated on Erin.

Scout lay between them, in front of the fire, his eyes closed as if he could finally relax for a little while. The dog's belly should be full, and the warmth of the fire seemed a welcome companion for all of them.

Erin set her coffee mug on the end table beside her. "I told you some basics earlier. But I guess what I didn't tell you is that Bella is adopted."

His eyebrows shot up. "Is she? I had no idea."

Erin nodded as memories flooded her. "She was ten when she came to live with me and Liam. An old friend from high school had a rough go at life and ended up in jail for quite a while. She personally asked me if I would adopt Bella, and, of course, I said yes."

"How did Liam feel about that?"

The day the adoption was finalized flashed back into her mind, replaying like an old film reel. "He was all in favor of it. At least, at first. But later, I couldn't help but wonder if he felt jealous."

Dillon narrowed his gaze. "Jealous because you were giving her more attention?"

Erin offered a half shrug. "Maybe. It never really made sense to me. I felt like I gave Liam plenty of attention. They both deserved all my attention, and I did the best that I could."

"It sounds like you're a good mom."

She shrugged, feeling another round of guilt wash through her. "Sometimes I don't know. If I was such a good mom, then why is Bella not here with me now?" Her voice broke.

Dillon leaned toward her. "Sometimes in life, there are things out of our control. You can try to be a helicopter parent all you want, but there comes a point when you have to realize that some things are out of our hands."

"That's hard to stomach when you try to play by the rules and do everything right. And sometimes you try to play by the rules and do everything right, and everything still goes desperately wrong." She swallowed hard, feeling a knot form in her throat.

"Do you believe in God, Erin?"

Dillon's question nearly startled her. But Erin quickly nodded. "I do. I more than believe in Him. I try to follow Him."

"Good. Because that faith will sustain you now. Hold tight to it. Know that we have hope, not only in the way things turn out in this life, but also in the eternal."

His words caused a burst of comfort to wash through her. It meant a lot to have someone here who understood, who could remind her of those important things in life.

"I've been trying to cling to my faith. But it's definitely being tested right now, to say the least."

"I'll continue to pray for you. I know that prayer has helped sustain me through some of my toughest and darkest moments also."

She wondered exactly what Dillon meant by that. It sounded like there was more to the story.

Before she could respond, her phone buzzed. She started, wondering if it was a text either from Bella or about Bella.

Quickly, she looked at the screen.

But the same unknown number from earlier popped up. Along with another cryptic message.

You bring destruction wherever you go.

A cry caught in her throat. Why was someone so determined to make a bad situation even worse? Why did they want to try and be her jury and judge?

"Erin..." Dillon looked at her with a questioning look in his eyes.

Before she could say anything, a creak sounded on her porch.

Scout suddenly stood, his body tense as he looked at the door and began to growl.

Was someone outside?

Could it be Bella?

Or was it someone who wanted to make Erin suffer for sins they only assumed she'd committed?

EIGHT

Dillon felt his muscles bristle.

"Stay here," he told Erin.

From the look on her face, she wasn't expecting anybody. Hope and grief seemed to clash in her gaze as she stared at the front of her house.

If somebody was here for a friendly visit, they would have knocked.

Dillon instructed Scout to stay beside Erin before pulling out his gun and creeping toward the door. He stood at the edge of it and flipped the curtain out of the way.

A shadowy figure paced outside.

What was someone doing out there? Coming to leave another message? To finish what he'd started when his attempt to push Erin off the cliff hadn't been successful?

Moving quietly so his presence wouldn't

be noticed, Dillon gripped his gun with one hand and the door handle with the other. He then threw the door open and stepped outside with his gun drawn.

"Freeze!" he ordered.

The man on the porch held up his hands. But there wasn't an apology in the intruder's gaze—only vengeance.

"Who are you?" the man demanded as he sneered at Dillon.

Dillon stared at the man. He didn't have the impression this guy was Erin's boyfriend or even a relative. Yet he seemed familiar with the house.

"I'm the one with the gun," Dillon said. "I suggest you answer that first."

The man narrowed his gaze. "I'm Arnold Lansing."

Realization hit Dillon. "You must be Liam's brother."

The man's scowl deepened. "That's right. Who are you?"

"I'm with the search and rescue crew. What are you doing here?"

"I came to see Erin. Do you have a problem

with that?" Anger edged into the man's voice as if he silently dared Dillon to defy him.

Before he could respond, Dillon heard a shuffle behind him, and Erin appeared. Based on her body language, she wasn't happy to see Arnold. Instead, she crossed her arms and glared at the man.

"You're not welcome here." Her voice hardened with every syllable.

Arnold bristled as he stared at her. "This was my brother's house. I'll always be welcome here."

"Your brother's not here right now," Dillon said. "So I would rethink those words. If the lady says you're not welcome, then you're not welcome."

"My brother bought this property with his own money." Arnold's voice rose as he jammed his foot onto the ground.

"He bought it while we were married. As soon as I'm able to sell it and move somewhere else so I can get away from these bad memories, I plan on doing just that."

"Now, what are you doing here?" Dillon asked as he stared at Arnold.

Arnold's gaze remained on Erin, still cold and calculated. "I heard about what you did to Bella."

Erin adamantly swung her head back and forth. "I didn't do anything to Bella. I'm desperate to find her. If you were any kind of uncle to her, you'd be out there with me helping with the search efforts."

"Just like you did with my brother?"

"You know good and well I did not do anything to your brother." Erin's voice sounded at just above a hiss. "Liam outweighed me by a hundred pounds at least. What exactly do you think I could have done to him?"

"You're smart. I'm sure you could figure out something."

Dillon had heard enough of this exchange. He stepped forward, placing himself between Arnold and Erin. "I think it's time for you to leave."

"What are you going to do?" Arnold let out a sardonic chuckle. "Call the police?"

Dillon felt himself revolt. Guys like this were the kind who gave cops a bad name.

And when one cop had a bad name, it damaged all cops.

"You need to go," Dillon repeated.

Arnold stared at Erin a moment longer before taking a step back. "Very well then. All the best. With everything. You're going to need it."

Dillon waited at the door until he saw the man drive away. Then he turned back to Erin.

What exactly was going on here?

There was clearly more to her story.

And the more he learned, the more he realized just how much danger she was in right now.

Erin pulled a blanket over herself but that didn't help her chill. The icy feeling came from down deep inside her.

As she rubbed her hands over her arms, she felt the scrapes on her palms from her fall down the cliff earlier today.

She was going to make it through this, just like Dillon had said. She just had to remember that her hope went beyond all these circumstances.

Dillon pulled his chair closer and sat in front of her, his studious gaze on her, worry rimming his eyes. "Are you okay, Erin?"

She nodded even though she felt anything but okay. Every part of her life had been shaken up, and she wasn't sure if she'd ever recover.

"Arnold's never really liked me that much, if you can't tell."

Dillon's regard darkened. "He has no right to treat you that way. How long has he been giving you a hard time?"

"Basically, from the moment we met. Who knows what Liam told him about me, for that matter."

"It doesn't sound like Liam treated you very well, either."

Erin shrugged, unable to fight the memories any longer. "He did at first. He was charming and sweet. But after we were married, that started to change. Then when we adopted Bella, it really changed. I was afraid he might lash out at her one day. As soon as I realized that was a possibility, I left him."

"I didn't realize that you were separated before he went missing."

"We were more than separated. We were divorced. And I got the house in the divorce, for the record."

Dillon leaned back, the thoughtful expression remaining on his face. "So why do people think that you're responsible for his disappearance?"

Erin rubbed her arms again and stared into the fire as more memories flooded her. "We were seen fighting the morning Liam disappeared. We got into a huge argument, and several people were around to hear it."

"How does that prove anything?"

"Apparently, in some people's minds, that means I did something to Liam. But I wouldn't have done that. Even though I don't always trust the legal system, I tried to go through the proper means of ending my relationship with him. Instead of enacting my own form of justice, I did everything the legal way instead."

"It doesn't sound like Liam was able to accept the terms of your divorce."

She stared into the fire, watching the flames dance. "He didn't want a divorce. But eventually he conceded, and it was finalized."

"How often does Arnold confront you like he did tonight?"

"It's random," Erin said. "I won't hear from him for months, and I'll think he's gone from my life. Then suddenly he'll show up, and I'll see him several times in a row."

Dillon frowned. "That's got to be hard."

"It is. I especially don't want Bella to have to see it or have any part of it. But Arnold even harassed her one time while she was at school."

Dillon seemed to stiffen. "What did he do?"

"He called to her through the fence at the school and told her that her mom was a killer. She was so upset…as you can probably imagine."

"That's terrible. Did you report it?"

Erin shrugged, no longer feeling disappointed in the local police. She'd simply accepted that they'd never be on her side. "No, it's like I said, the police believe I did something to Liam. They don't care about anything that I have to say."

"That's a shame. I'm sorry that you're having to go through all of this."

The sincerity of his words made Erin flush. "I appreciate that. But I suppose that I made my bed and now I have to sleep in it, as the saying goes. My friends never really liked Liam. Told me that I shouldn't marry him. I thought I knew better. And now look at me."

She wanted to laugh, but she couldn't. It wasn't a laughing matter.

Liam had slowly separated her from all those friends who hadn't wanted her to be with Liam. He'd told her lies about them. Told her they were just jealous. Eventually, in order to preserve her marriage, she'd pulled away from them.

Which was exactly what Liam had wanted. She'd become isolated, with no one to talk to and no one to support her.

In other words, she'd been trapped and hopeless.

But adopting Bella had changed that.

"We all make mistakes," Dillon said. "What

about that text you got right before we heard someone outside? What was that about?"

Erin found the message on her phone and showed it to him. His eyes widened as he read the words *You bring destruction wherever you go*.

"What an odd message for someone to send you," he muttered.

"What am I going to do, Dillon?" She heard the desperation in her voice, but she couldn't take it back. The emotion was raw—but it was true.

"First thing in the morning, we're going to get the search parties together again and we're going to look for Bella. We're not going to give up until we find her."

She let his words sink in and slowly nodded. "Okay then. But I doubt I'm going to get any rest tonight."

Dillon frowned before saying, "How would you feel if I slept on your couch? I just don't want to see any trouble come back here. Besides, the roads are bad, and it's late."

"I'm sure you have a life outside of this." His offer was kind, but he'd already done so much for her. Gone above and beyond. Done so much more than anyone could reasonably expect.

"I'm not married," Dillon explained. "And I have somebody who can help me with the dogs back at my place. My nephew lives there. I'll give him a call."

She nibbled on the inside of her lip for a moment as she contemplated his offer. "Are you sure this won't be too much trouble?"

"I'm sure. In fact, I'd feel a lot better if you'd let me stay."

Erin stared at him another moment before nodding. This was no time to let her pride get in the way. Dillon staying here answered a lot of prayers.

"Okay," she finally said. "Thank you. I owe you big-time for this."

His gaze locked with hers. "You don't owe me anything."

Erin had brought Dillon a pillow and blanket so he could sleep on the couch. But he knew he wouldn't be getting much rest tonight. He had too much on his mind.

He paced toward the front window again and glanced outside at Erin's front yard. He had a strange feeling they were being watched right now.

Had the person who'd taken Bella come back to see what Erin was doing? Was this all out of some sort of twisted revenge against the schoolteacher?

What about Arnold? Could he be behind this? If Liam had resented Erin for adopting Bella, maybe Arnold wanted to give Erin some payback by taking Bella away from her now. Dillon wasn't sure if his theory had any validity, but he kept it in the back of his mind.

Scout stood from near the fireplace and paced over to him. The dog appeared more triggered than usual as he panted and seemed like he couldn't settle down.

Scout knew something was going on, didn't he?

Dillon thought about going outside to check things himself. But he knew that wouldn't be wise.

He didn't know what he was up against nor did he know this landscape. He was better off staying inside and being prepared for whatever might come. If anyone got too close to the house, Scout would alert him.

Instead, he decided to make a few phone calls about tomorrow's search and rescue mission. But first, he checked the weather. The snow was supposed to let up and pass by then.

Still, that didn't change the fact that everything was going to be covered in a layer of the icy precipitation. After what had happened today, they were going to need to be very careful. Not only would the trails be dangerous, so would the drive to get there.

Dillon glanced at the time and saw it wasn't quite midnight. Still, he knew Rick was a night owl. He called him to get a quick update on what happened today. Besides, Dillon could use someone to talk to, to bounce ideas off of.

"It took you longer to call than I thought it would," Rick answered.

"It's been a busy day. Any updates since we last talked?"

"I wish there were. But no, not yet. If the weather allows, we'll go back out tomorrow and keep searching the trails for Bella," Rick said. "We don't want too many volunteers in the forest right now because of the icy conditions. It could be dangerous."

That didn't surprise Dillon. They didn't want to add another tragedy to an already tense situation. "What about a helicopter?"

"We have one lined up to use tomorrow. How did it go with Scout? Did he stay on the trail?"

Dillon's mind drifted back to the moment they'd had to turn around. "I felt like we were so close to finding Bella today when we had to go back."

"It was a good thing you did because conditions got even worse. It was bad out there with the temperatures dropping so quickly." Rick paused. "I guess you know who she is now."

Erin's face flashed through his mind. "I do. But that doesn't change anything."

"I just want you to be careful."

"You actually think she did something to Liam Lansing?" Dillon honestly wanted to know his friend's opinion.

"I never cared for the man much myself,"

Rick said. "But a lot of people suspected her. You know the spouse or the ex is always one of the first people considered in an investigation like that one."

"It sounds to me like people in town didn't like her and wanted a reason to find her guilty."

"The community bonds are strong in Boone's Hollow," Rick said. "Everyone loved Liam, but Erin was still an outsider. I also know that Liam had a way of getting people on his side. Who knows what the truth is? It's usually somewhere in the middle."

"Usually. But sometimes that's not the case. Sometimes the truth squarely rests on one person's shoulders and not the other's."

"I can't argue with that."

"What about Blackstone?" Dillon continued. "Do you trust him?"

"I try not to deal with the man unless I absolutely have to."

That said it all as far as Dillon was concerned.

"Listen, I'm still filling out all this paperwork, but we're going to meet at 8:00 a.m. so we can start our search efforts again," Rick said. "Send me the quadrants where Scout last picked up on Bella's scent, and we'll start there. I'll send you more information first thing in the morning. Sound like a plan?"

"That sounds great. I have a feeling Erin will be coming along, too."

Rick didn't say anything for a moment. "Are you sure that's a good idea?"

"I'm sure I won't be able to keep her away. She's determined to find Bella—either with us or on her own. On her own, she might get herself killed."

"Okay then. As long as you know what you're getting into."

Did Dillon know what he was getting into? He wasn't sure.

But he wasn't going to change his mind now.

NINE

As Erin rode in the Jeep with Dillon and Scout the next morning, she prayed that today would be successful.

She'd hardly gotten any sleep last night as she'd prayed those words over and over. Prayer was the only thing she could rely on right now. Not only that, prayer was also the best thing she could do right now.

She needed to trust in God because He was the only one who could get her through this situation.

She'd heard Dillon on the phone last night. Heard him pacing. Heard Scout bark a couple of times.

When she'd asked Dillon about it this morning, he'd shrugged her question off. But she had a feeling that someone else had been outside her place last night.

Had Arnold come back? Had another member of Liam's family come by to make their presence known?

She had no idea.

She only knew that today was probably going to be just as treacherous as yesterday had been. Erin had tried to mentally prepare herself for that fact, but she wasn't sure she'd succeeded.

"The search and rescue team is hoping to get the copter out today." Dillon's calm voice cut through the silence.

A helicopter? Maybe that would find something. "That would be good."

"Even though it seems like winter is a bad time to get lost—and it is—the good news is that without all the leaves on the trees, it's much easier to see things from the sky."

She supposed that could be a good thing.

She crossed her arms as she glanced at him again. "Is law enforcement still treating this as if Bella has run away?"

"My understanding is that they're exploring both options—that she could have run or that she could have been abducted. Until they have confirmation, that's what they'll continue to do."

"What about that second set of footprints?"

"It indicates she could have met someone. But that still doesn't mean she was abducted."

Erin rubbed her throat, knowing she couldn't argue with him. He was absolutely correct.

"Besides, if someone snatched her, you would have probably received a ransom call by now." Dillon glanced at her before turning his gaze back onto the road.

"I don't have money. I thought cases like that usually involved wealthy people."

"Sometimes, but not always."

"I just worry that someone abducted her, and that person has her in a car right now and is taking her as far away from this area as possible." Erin's voice cracked as emotions tried to bubble to the surface.

"That's a call that Rick and Blackstone will need to make. I know it's hard to trust Blackstone. We can go above him, if necessary."

Erin did a double take at him. "If you go above him, there's no way they're going to hire you to work search and rescue anymore. You'll be blacklisted in this town."

He shrugged. "Sometimes that's the cost of doing what's right."

"I don't want to cost you your career."

Dillon glanced at her. "I appreciate your concern, but I assure you that I can handle myself."

She nodded and stared out the window, feeling like every minute that passed, the mess around her grew. It was bad enough that Liam's disappearance had upended Erin's life. But now Dillon was willing to risk his career for this.

She admired the man for his stance, but she hated to think of more innocent people getting caught in the cross fire.

Finally, they reached the parking area near the trailhead. This time, no one had followed them, nor had Erin received any more threatening text messages. She took that as a good sign.

A brush of nerves swept through her as she climbed from the Jeep and merged with the rest of the search and rescue operation. Several new people had joined the team, people Erin assumed were volunteers, based on their clothing. A few people sent her strange glances.

Did they think she was guilty?

Erin knew there was a good chance the answer to that question was yes.

But she had to push past those opinions and keep her focus on finding Bella. That was the only thing that mattered.

She prayed that today would be successful. That today would be the day they found Bella. Her daughter had been missing for almost forty-eight hours now.

That was enough time for someone to have taken her far away from here.

Bile rose in Erin's stomach at the thought.

What if Bella was never found?

Dillon and Scout led the way down the icy trail. This was going to be trickier than he would have liked. But he knew time was of the essence right now.

More people had shown up to help search— but only experienced SAR volunteers.

They'd been divided into six different groups so they could cover more of the area. Dillon, Scout and Erin were on one team. Right now, they walked with Rick and two other rangers—Dan and William.

Later on, further down the trail, they would split up, but for now they all headed in the same direction.

It had been good to see the volunteers who wanted to help. The more of this wilderness they could cover, the better.

The teams threaded their way through the woods back toward the area where they'd been last night, the spot where the trailhead split and where Scout had lost Bella's scent.

Dillon had already decided that he would head down into the valley—that was unless Scout somehow picked up Bella's scent again.

He knew there were a few old hunting cabins out here and had to wonder if maybe the girl had somehow gotten inside one of those.

But this wilderness was so vast. Someone had gotten lost here one time and a search party had come out looking for him for two weeks, to no avail. People didn't realize how dangerous these mountains could be until they were in the middle of them. By then, it was usually too late.

Of course, Dillon didn't tell Erin that. She was dealing with enough harsh realities without him adding to her burdens.

As he glanced behind him, he noted that Erin was being a real trooper as she kept up with them. She wasn't complaining, though she was breathing heavy.

"How long have you had Scout?" she asked after she seemed to notice him glance back at her.

"Four years," he said. "Someone left him at the pound. As soon as I saw him, I knew he had to come home with me."

"Is it normal for dogs from the pound to become search and rescue dogs?"

He climbed over a downed tree before reaching back to also help Erin across. "They make the best search and rescue dogs, I'd say. Those dogs know they've been rescued and they just want to give back."

"That's really beautiful."

"It's true."

It was cold out here and slippery. Nothing about it was enjoyable. But it was necessary.

When they got to the area of the path where it split, Dillon nodded toward the trail leading into the valley. "This is where we part ways."

Rick nodded. "We need to stay in touch and make sure that everybody stays safe. Clearly, these conditions are treacherous, to say the least."

"We'll be careful," Dillon said. "And we'll be in touch if we need you."

With one final nod to each other, he, Scout and Erin began their descent into the valley.

He paused near a particularly rocky portion of the trail and held out his hand to help Erin down. As her hand slipped into his, a shock of electricity coursed through him.

Electricity? That made no sense.

He wasn't interested in dating or anything romantic. After his engagement had ended last year, he'd written off love for good. His fiancée had decided she couldn't handle a rough patch, and she'd left him.

He quickly released Erin's hand and they continued along the trail.

Just as they reached a relatively flat area, a new sound cracked the air.

Gunfire.

"Get down!" Dillon shouted.

He turned toward Erin, hoping he wasn't too late.

Erin ducked behind a boulder as another bullet flew through the air.

Why in the world was someone shooting at them? Was it a mistake? Had they been caught in a hunter's cross fire?

No, those bullets had been purposeful, Erin realized.

Someone *wanted* to hurt them.

Was it the same person who'd abducted Bella? If so, why would this person come after Erin and Dillon now?

So much didn't make sense.

"Stay down." Dillon crouched with Scout across the trail behind another boulder.

As he said the words, another bullet split the bark on the tree in front of the boulder.

Erin pressed her lips together, determined not to scream and give the shooter any satisfaction. But her pulse pounded in her ears and she could hardly breathe.

When would this nightmare end?

She glanced at Dillon again and saw he'd withdrawn his gun.

Her pulse pounded even faster.

As he held the weapon in one hand, he pulled out a radio with his other hand and called in what was happening. Erin assumed Rick and his team were a considerable distance away at this point. She was just thankful the radio was working. Her cell phone had no service out here.

She had no idea how this situation was going to end up playing out.

"He's getting closer." Dillon slipped his radio back onto his belt and peered around the boulder. "We're going to need to move."

Erin froze. The last thing she wanted to do was to move. She felt safe behind the rock—at least, she felt safer here than she did running.

But she needed to trust Dillon's advice right now.

As another bullet rang through the air, she realized she had no other choice.

She glanced over at Dillon again and he nodded at the trail in the distance. "That path will be our best bet. It's going to be slippery, and you'll need to watch your step."

Erin nodded, trying to process everything that was happening and keep her head in the game.

"I'm going to stay behind you," Dillon continued. "Whatever you need to do, remember that we need to keep moving."

She nodded, but her brain felt numb, almost as if she even attempted to process all this, it would shut down.

Was this what Bella had gone through also?

She held back another cry, unable to think about that.

"Let's move," Dillon said. "We don't have any more time to waste."

As he said the words, another bullet pierced the air and Erin gasped. This guy wasn't letting up.

She wanted to peer over the rock, to see who it was and where the bullets were coming from. But she didn't dare.

As Dillon ran toward her, she rose from her

hiding spot and darted down the slippery trail. Her breath came out in short, wispy gasps that immediately iced in the frigid air.

The first part of the trail was manageable. But as the path turned rocky *and* icy, her shoes practically skated on the slippery surface beneath her.

She hesitated, trying to keep her footing.

As she did, she felt another bullet whiz by. She sucked in a breath.

The bullet had practically skimmed her hair. It was that close.

This guy was following them, wasn't he? Hunting them?

He wouldn't stop until they were dead.

Erin held back a cry at the thought of it.

"You can do this, Erin," Dillon said behind her. "You just need to keep moving."

She didn't have the energy to respond. Instead, she kept walking, just as Dillon told her.

The ground in this area wasn't only icy, but the rocks were uneven. The terrain would be hard to navigate on a nice day when they weren't running for their lives. Today, it almost felt impossible.

You can do it, she told herself.

Erin kept moving...and moving...and moving.

As another bullet cracked the air, she sprang into action and darted forward. As she did, her foot caught on a rock. Her ankle twisted.

She gasped as she fell to the ground.

"Erin!" Dillon muttered as he rushed toward her.

She'd sprained her ankle, hadn't she? The pain coursing through her seemed to confirm her fears.

Despair built deep inside her.

No...not now.

Dear Lord...

How was she going to get out of this one?

TEN

Dillon leaned over Erin, trying to shield her from any oncoming bullets.

But this didn't look good. The way she grasped her ankle made it clear she was in pain.

He'd known it wasn't safe to run around in these elements. But the gunman had left them little choice.

Another bullet split the air behind them before hitting the ground several feet away.

Erin gasped as her eyes lit with fear.

Dillon leaned closer. "Can you put any pressure on your ankle?"

"Let me see." With Dillon's help, Erin tried to stand, but she nearly crumpled back onto the ground as soon as any weight hit her ankle.

Dillon was going to need to think of a way to get them out of the situation—and quickly.

Footsteps sounded—closer this time.

He gripped his gun and peered around the boulder.

He didn't want to use his weapon—but he would if he had to.

When he saw a figure dressed in black raise his gun, Dillon had no choice but to raise his own weapon. He quickly lined up his target and fired.

The bullet hit the man's shoulder and he let out a groan.

Dillon had just bought them some time— he didn't know how much.

That wound would slow the man down, but wouldn't necessarily stop him.

Dillon turned back to Erin. "I'm going to put my arm around you and help you down the rest of this trail. Then we're going to find shelter. We're going to get through this, okay?"

She glanced up at him, fear welling in her gaze. She nodded anyway.

Dillon slipped his arm around her waist. He let go of Scout's leash and let the dog walk in front of them. Then he helped Erin along the treacherous path.

He still held his gun in his other hand, and he craned his neck behind him, looking for any signs of danger.

There was nothing.

Not at the moment.

He needed to find one of those old cabins he'd been thinking about earlier. A cabin would offer them shelter from the elements and protection from this gunman—for a little while, at least.

The only thing that protected them right now were the bends and curves of the trail. Plus, the gunman seemed to have slowed down.

Erin drew in deep, labored breaths as they continued down the path. Dillon had to give her props, however. She was doing her best to keep moving.

"You're doing just fine," he assured her.

She nodded, but still looked unconvinced.

Dillon stole a quick glance behind him and thought he saw a flash of movement. Was that the gunman?

It was his best guess.

He knew that Rick and Benjamin were on their way right now. But he had little hope they'd get there in time.

As Dillon glanced ahead, he thought he saw a structure in the distance.

Was that one of the cabins he vaguely remembered being out here?

Going inside might buy them a little time. Plus, the structure would give them a place to hunker down until backup arrived. Erin needed to take some weight off her ankle.

"Do you see what I see?" Hope lilted in Erin's voice.

"That's where we're headed. Do you think you can make it?"

"I'll do my best," she said. "I'm sorry that I'm slowing you down."

"It's not your fault. You were only doing what I told you."

He kept his arm around her and helped her navigate the terrain. She let out little gasps, obviously in pain. But she kept going, kept moving. Her determination was admirable.

They continued over the rocky, uneven trail.

At least it was flatter here, with no cliffs now that they were closer to the valley.

As the cabin neared, Dillon observed the small structure. It was probably less than five hundred square feet. Trees grew all around it, and junk had been left around the foundation—wood and cinderblocks and buckets, even a ladder.

Scout ran ahead and climbed onto the porch, almost as if he knew exactly what Dillon wanted him to do.

Moving as quickly as possible, Dillon climbed to the front door and pulled on it.

But it was locked.

He let out a breath.

Now they had to figure out plan B.

As Scout growled at something in the distance, Dillon realized they had no time to waste.

The gunman was getting closer and they were running out of time.

"Dillon?" Erin's voice trembled despite her wishes to stay strong.

"Give me a second," he muttered as he glanced around.

She couldn't believe they'd made it this far only to find the door was locked. What were they going to do now?

Certainly the gunman was getting closer and closer. What would the man do once he was near enough to shoot them point-blank?

A chill washed through her.

She couldn't bear to think about it.

And her ankle…she wished it didn't throb like it did. She wished she could put weight on it. But every time she tried, she nearly collapsed.

"I hate to do this but…" Dillon reached down and picked up an old board from the ground.

In one motion, he thrust it into the window and broke the glass. Using the same board, he cleared the shards from around the edges. Then he turned to her.

"You're going to have to climb through this."

Erin nodded, trying to imagine how that was going to happen. But this was no time to overthink things. She just needed to move.

Using his hands, Dillon boosted her through the window. She slid inside and landed on the couch below the window. A moment later, Dillon lifted Scout inside before climbing through himself.

Once he was inside, he didn't miss a beat. He paced to the center of the room and surveyed the area. "I need to get you away from these windows."

Moving quickly, he went to the kitchen table and turned it over. He then helped Erin behind it.

She nestled between the cabinets and table with her knees pulled to her chest. Scout lay beside her, almost as if the canine sensed she needed comfort. She reached over and rubbed his fur, grateful that the dog was here now.

She heard Dillon moving in the other part of the room and something scraped across the floor. Was he moving furniture?

A moment later, Dillon sat beside her, his gun drawn and his posture showing he was on guard.

Her heart pounded in her chest.

Would they have a shootout? She hoped that

wasn't the case. But certainly Dillon was preparing for what could be the worst-case scenario.

She continued to rub Scout's head as she waited for whatever was going to unfold.

As she did, her thoughts wandered. She remembered what Dillon had said to her when they'd reached the cabin. When he'd assured her that this wasn't her fault and that she had done her best.

The words had brought such an unusual comfort—an unusual comfort that surprised even her.

Liam…he would have lashed out at her. Told her everything was her fault. Blamed the situation on her and put it all on her shoulders.

It was what Erin was used to and what she'd been prepared to hear. But hearing the compassionate and rational words from Dillon reminded her that there were still good people in this world.

Not every man was like Liam—thank goodness.

"Are you still doing okay?" Dillon glanced over at her.

Erin nodded, probably a little too quickly. "I think so. What can I do?"

"Stay low and stay by Scout. I'll do the rest."

"But what if the gunman comes...?"

He locked gazes with her. "I'm just taking each moment as it comes."

Just as he said the words, a creak sounded outside.

Was the gunman on the porch?

Fear shot through her.

What was going to happen next?

Dillon's muscles tensed as he waited.

The gunman was clearly here. Even Scout sensed someone's presence. The dog's fur rose.

Dillon grasped his gun as he aimed it over the table, waiting to strike.

This wasn't the way he'd wanted things to play out. All he'd wanted was to find Bella. To make sure that the girl was okay. Now, somehow, it had turned into a confrontation.

He'd been in situations like this before. He'd trained to handle himself during standoffs.

As much as he'd like to believe there would always be a positive outcome, he knew that wasn't the case. One of his colleagues had been killed in a bank robbery a few years ago. That event had reminded him of the fragility of life.

Dillon didn't intend to share his thoughts with Erin. Not now.

She was already scared and on the verge of breaking, and he didn't want to add to that.

He waited, holding his breath as he prepared himself for whatever would happen. A shadow moved across one of the windows.

He'd moved a bookshelf in front of the broken window in the hope of slowing whoever was outside. If it were Rick or another ranger, they would have most likely announced themselves already.

That only left the gunman.

Dillon glanced around the small cabin. A loft stretched above them. There were four windows total. One by the bookshelf. One the shadow had crossed. And two other smaller windows on either side of the cabin.

Those two would be difficult to get to because the deck didn't span the sides of the cabin, which would make them harder to access.

So what kind of play would this guy make next?

"Dillon?" Erin sounded breathless as she said his name.

He put a finger over his lips, motioning for her to be quiet. Instead, she began to rub Scout's fur again.

The footsteps stopped.

What exactly was the man planning now? Did he have other tricks up his sleeve?

Dillon's heart thrummed in his ear.

He thought he'd put these high-octane days behind him. But part of him would always be a cop. It almost seemed ingrained in him.

Quiet continued to stretch outside.

Dillon wished he knew what the man was doing. What he was planning. Why he was after them.

Was this person who'd abducted Bella now determined to kill Erin? Why? Why abduct Bella first?

The details just didn't make any sense to him. But he'd need to figure that out later.

A new sound filled the air.

A creak.

This time, it came from the direction of the bookcase.

Did this guy know that they had come inside?

The gunman had been close enough that it wouldn't surprise Dillon if the man had seen them, if he'd spotted the broken window. Plus, he, Erin and Scout had no doubt left tracks in the snow, which would make it easier to follow them.

Dillon gripped his gun, still pointing it in the direction of the front door and the window beside it. Still bracing himself for the worst.

He heard another noise. It almost sounded like wood scraping against the floor.

The next instant, the bookcase crashed to the ground and a bullet fired inside.

ELEVEN

Erin swallowed back a scream.

The man was here.

And he was going to kill them.

She ducked and buried her face again, pulling Scout closer.

As she did, she heard Dillon fire. The smell of ammo filled the room and more fear clutched her heart.

How were they ever going to get out of this alive?

She began to pray furiously. *Dear Lord, help us! Protect us! All I want is to find Bella. She's the only thing that's important. But I need to stay alive in order to do that.*

More bullets flew and she heard wood splintering behind her.

Dillon fired back again.

How much ammo had he brought with him? How long could he hold this guy off?

Erin had no idea. There was nowhere else to hide.

The gunfire paused for another moment.

She held her breath, anticipating the man's next move. Waiting for more gunfire.

But there was nothing.

Her heart thumped so loudly that she was certain Dillon and Scout could hear the *thump, thump, thumps.*

Scout raised his head, almost as if he were also curious about what was going on.

Had the gunman regrouped? Was he headed to another part of the cabin to fire on them from a different angle or take them by surprise?

Dillon's thoughts seemed to mirror hers. "Stay low," he murmured.

He still grasped the gun, and his shoulders looked tight. At least if Erin was stuck out here, she was with Dillon and not alone. If she'd been on her own, she'd most certainly be dead right now.

No more gunfire sounded…not yet.

But another sound filled the air.

What was that?

The noise was faint but getting louder by the moment.

Had the man planned something else? Was more danger headed their way as they sat there unassuming?

"Dillon?" Erin's voice cracked with fear.

"I hear it, too," he muttered.

A moment later, the sound became more clear.

Whomp, whomp, whomp.

Erin released her breath.

If she wasn't mistaken, that was a helicopter.

Was it from the search and rescue mission?

Even more so, had the sound scared the gunman away?

She hoped and prayed that was the case.

Just as the thought crossed her mind, she glanced at the floor and her breath caught.

She reached forward and picked up a pink scrunchie—one that had images of a laughing cat on it.

"Erin?"

"This is Bella's."

* * *

The rescue crew had found a clearing to land in. Another ranger met them there and had taken Dillon, Scout and Erin to a local hospital to have Erin's ankle checked while the rest of the team searched the cabin for evidence and the woods for the gunman.

Had someone snatched Bella and taken her to that cabin? Or had she wandered there by herself? It was still a possibility that she hadn't been abducted; that she'd just run.

They had too many questions and not enough answers at this point.

Dillon waited outside Erin's room, Scout beside him, until the doctor okayed her to leave. Surprise stretched across her face when she stepped out and spotted him in the hallway.

"Dillon...you didn't have to wait." She leaned down and patted Scout's head. "You, either, boy."

"How did you plan on getting home then?" Dillon raised an eyebrow, trying to add some levity to the situation.

Erin let out a sheepish laugh. "Good point.

But really, I feel like I've turned your life upside down, and you don't even know me."

He shrugged, trying not to make a big deal of his decision. "You didn't ask me to do any of this, so you have no reason to feel guilty. How about if I give you a ride?"

"Is your Jeep even here?" More confusion rolled over her features.

"I had one of the rangers bring it by for me while the doctor was treating you." He paused. "I hope I didn't overstep, but I also had someone tow your car from the lot. My friend Darrel is going to take it into his shop and replace the tires for you."

"That was so thoughtful of you. Thank you." She offered a grateful smile.

Dillon glanced at her foot, which was now in a walking cast. "How are you?"

"The doctor said it's just a sprain. He wrapped it, and I can put a little weight on it for now. Nothing too strenuous."

"That's good news at least." They could both use some good news considering the events of the past twenty-four hours.

"It is." Erin paused and shoved her hands

into her pockets as she turned to address him. "Thank you so much for everything that you did today."

He stared at her a moment. Stared at the lovely lines of her face. Her expressive eyes. The grief that seemed to tug at her lips.

He hadn't expected to be impressed. He'd expected a grieving, panic-stricken mother.

She was those things—of course. It would be strange if she wasn't.

But she also had a quiet strength, an unwavering determination, and a fragile vulnerability. She'd been given an unfair hand. She didn't deserve the scrutiny people had put her under. She needed the community's support right now.

She might not get that support from her neighbors now, but she would get it from him.

He rubbed his throat before saying, "I'm sorry we haven't been able to find Bella yet."

Erin's lips tugged into a frown. "Me, too. The more time that passes, the less the chances are that we're going to find her. I've watched enough TV shows to know that."

She sniffled, as if holding back a sob.

He wanted to reach out to her. To offer her some comfort. To tell her everything would be okay.

Instead, he settled on saying, "Don't give up hope."

"I'm trying not to." She ran a hand across her brow. "I really am."

Dillon nodded to the elevator in the distance. "Are you ready to go?"

"I am. More than ready to go, for that matter."

They silently started toward the elevator. There wasn't much to say. Dillon was still processing exactly what had happened. It would take a while to comprehend the scope of the danger they were in.

He helped Erin and Scout into his Jeep and then cranked the engine. He felt like there were things that he wanted to say, he just wasn't exactly sure what those things were.

Part of him wanted to apologize, even though he knew none of this was his fault. But the situation had to be frustrating for her. Now it was already later in the afternoon.

They'd have to wait until tomorrow to search again.

"Are there any updates in the search for Bella?" Erin looked up at him, her eyes glimmering with hope.

He somberly shook his head. "I wish there were. But there's no new news."

She frowned again. "I checked my phone just in case there were any messages. I didn't have service in the mountains, but part of me hoped someone had left a message. Maybe Bella. Or, if she was abducted, then from the person who took her. The silence is maddening."

Against his better judgment, he reached over and squeezed her hand. "I know this has to be really hard on you. I'm sorry."

Erin glanced at his hand as it covered hers before offering a quick smile. "Thank you."

Scout barked in the back of the Jeep.

"I think Scout agrees with me."

Her smile widened. "He's a good dog."

Dillon pulled his hand back and gripped the gearshift.

Immediately, he missed the soft feel of her skin.

He cleared his throat and turned his attention to Scout instead.

"You're getting hungry, aren't you, boy?" Dillon murmured.

Erin glanced back at the dog and rubbed his head. "Do we need to stop and get him something?"

"I packed some food for him, but I *am* out now."

"Do what you need to do. Scout is a hero as far as I'm concerned."

He stole another glance at her. "Are you sure you don't mind if we swing by my place?"

"Not at all," Erin said. "I'm in no hurry to get back home. Who knows what's waiting for me there?"

Dillon let her words sink in before nodding. "Okay then. I'll make sure that this doesn't take long."

Erin's eyes lit up as she stared at Dillon's home.

The mountain farm was complete with an

old homestead and several outbuildings. With snow covering the property, it looked like a winter wonderland. No neighbors were visible for miles, just trees and gentle slopes.

The property looked like a slice of heaven.

"This is amazing," Erin said as she stepped from his Jeep.

Dillon climbed out and paused beside her. "I like it. It's my place where I can get away."

"Everybody needs a place like that, don't they?"

Scout barked in reply, and Dillon and Erin shared a smile.

Dillon nodded at a building in the distance. "How about I give you a quick tour?"

"I'd love one."

As they walked, Dillon held out his arm to offer some additional support. Normally, Erin might have refused, but not this time. This time, the last thing she needed was to sprain her other ankle or hurt herself in some other way.

Plus, she liked his touch.

When he'd touched her hand in the Jeep,

she'd felt her insides go still. She'd liked it a little too much.

And that realization terrified her.

She wasn't interested in dating again, and she certainly wasn't interested in dating a cop again—or a former cop.

But she had to remind herself that not every cop was like Liam, despite what her emotions told her.

They walked toward a barnlike building. She wasn't sure what to expect inside. But when Dillon opened the door, various dog kennels and barking canines greeted her in the finished, heated space.

As soon as he closed the door behind them, warmth surrounded Erin—a welcome relief from the brittle cold outside. Dillon released Scout from his lead and let him run free. He stopped and greeted each of the dogs in their luxury-sized runs.

"These are the dogs I train," he explained.

Erin walked down the center aisle, peering at each dog as she did. They appeared to be remarkably cared for and happy.

"They all look amazing." She paused beside a husky and rubbed the soft fur.

"They are. They're working dogs. But they enjoy what they do, and they're good at it."

Erin straightened and turned toward Dillon. "It's good to do something that you love."

"Yes, it is," he said. "Do you enjoy your job as a teacher?"

Dillon's question surprised her. He hadn't gotten personal with her. Yet, in some ways, she felt like she'd known this man much longer than she actually had.

She thought about his question a moment before answering. "I do. I love working with kids. I feel like it's my calling in life." She glanced up at him. "How about you?"

"Same here. As soon as I started training canines, I knew that this is what I should be doing."

"Do you like doing this more than you liked being a cop?"

His face instantly sobered. "Maybe. It's different. I get to help people through this job. That's what I like most about it."

She smiled. "That makes sense. Now, let me meet these guys."

For the next half hour, Dillon took her kennel by kennel and introduced her to the various dogs inside. She rubbed each of their heads and talked to them for a few minutes.

This place seemed like a fantasy getaway to her. She couldn't even imagine what it would be like to live here. Bella would love this.

Her daughter loved animals even more than Erin did. In fact, she'd been asking lately if they could get a dog, but Erin had told her not now. With Erin teaching eight hours a day and having to drive forty-minutes to and from work, it just wouldn't be possible to give a dog the attention it would need.

Dillon paused once they reached the other side of the building and pointed to the outside door behind him. "Listen, do you mind if I run inside a moment?"

"Not at all."

As they stepped toward the door, it suddenly opened and a shadowy figure stood there.

Erin gasped and stepped back.

Was it the gunman? Had he returned to finish what he'd started earlier?

TWELVE

"Carson," Dillon said.

He instinctively felt Erin's fear and pushed her behind him.

But it was just his nephew.

As Carson stepped into the light, his features came into view. The boy was seventeen, with thick, dark hair and an easy smile.

"Erin, this is my nephew, Carson. Carson, this is Erin Lansing. Carson helps me take care of the dogs, especially when I'm gone like I have been."

Erin's hand went over her heart as if it still pounded faster than necessary after Carson's surprise appearance. "Of course. It's great to meet you."

Carson nodded at her. "Same here. Any success today looking for that girl?"

"Unfortunately, no," Dillon said. "But it's Erin's daughter who's missing."

Dillon knew he needed to put that information out there before Carson asked any questions that might come across as insensitive.

Carson's face instantly stilled with reverence. "I'm really sorry to hear about your daughter, ma'am."

"Thank you," Erin said. "I appreciate that."

"Wait…your last name is Lansing?" Carson asked. "Is your daughter Bella?"

A knot formed between Erin's eyes. "She is. You know her?"

"Not well, but we've met a few times. Have you talked to Grayson yet?" Carson stared at her, looking genuinely curious.

"Who's Grayson?" The knot on Erin's brow became more defined.

Carson's eyes widened as if he realized he'd said something he shouldn't have. He stepped back, almost as if he wanted to snatch his words back. He opened his mouth but quickly shut it again.

"Carson, who is Grayson?" Dillon repeated.

"I'm sorry, I thought you knew." Carson

swallowed hard, his Adam's apple bobbing up and down.

"Knew what?" Erin's voice cracked with emotion, as if she were on the brink of tears.

"I've seen Bella around a few times at some football games between my school and hers. She's been hanging out with Grayson Davis."

Dillon sucked in a breath. He knew who Grayson Davis was. The whole family was trouble.

"What aren't you telling me?" Erin stared at Dillon, questions haunting her eyes.

"It's probably nothing." Dillon didn't want to alarm Erin for no reason. "I just know that Grayson's dad and grandfather—and even a couple of uncles—have been in prison before."

Erin's face seemed to fall with disappointment, and she squeezed the skin between her eyes. "What?"

He resisted the urge to reach out and try to comfort her again. That might be too much, too fast. "That doesn't mean he has anything to do with this. But you had no idea?"

She swung her head back and forth. "No,

I even asked Bella if she liked anyone. She rolled her eyes and stared and told me there was no one."

"It's not unusual for teens to want to keep information like this from their parents," Dillon said before looking back at Carson. "Is there anything else that you know?"

"No, just that she was hanging out with Grayson." Carson shrugged. "I'm sorry I can't be more help."

"You're doing just fine, Carson," Dillon said. "But if you hear anything else, please let us know."

"Of course. Whatever I can do." The boy nodded, his gaze unwavering and assuring them he'd keep his promise.

"Let's get you inside." Dillon put his hand on Erin's back to guide her toward the door. "Then we'll figure out our next plan of action."

Erin followed Dillon into his home, yet he couldn't help but note that her eyes looked determined. He knew exactly what she was thinking. She wanted to go talk to Grayson Davis herself.

That could turn into an ugly situation.

They desperately needed answers before Erin did something she might regret.

How could Bella have been seeing someone and not told her? When had this happened? When had Erin's relationship with her daughter turned from easygoing and conversational to a bond riddled with secrets?

The questions wouldn't stop pounding inside her head until finally an ache formed at her temples.

She wanted her daughter back. She wanted her *old* daughter back. She wanted to turn back time and somehow erase this mess, this heartache.

"I know what you're thinking." Dillon's voice pulled her from her thoughts.

She jerked her head up as he stepped into the kitchen from the back hallway.

She leaned her hip against the counter there and waited.

Normally, she'd be curious about his house or pictures on the fridge or the slight scent of evergreen permeating the air. But right now she could only think about Bella.

Erin stared up at Dillon. He'd claimed to know what she was thinking. "What's that?"

His gaze locked with hers. "That you want to talk to Grayson."

She crossed her arms, feeling a wave of defensiveness. "Can you blame me?"

Dillon shook his head, his perceptive eyes warm with compassion—and absent of the judgment she'd come to expect.

"Not at all," he murmured. "I'd say we should leave it to the police, but I'm beginning to think that's not such a great idea."

Erin released a breath she hadn't even realized she'd been holding. It felt so good to have someone who actually sounded like he was on her side.

"I'm going to leave Scout here with Carson, so he can rest. But if you'd like to go speak to Grayson, I'd like to go with you."

"You would do that for me?" Surprise lilted her voice.

"Of course. I'd want someone to do this for me if I were in your shoes."

Gratitude rushed through her, so warm and all-encompassing, it nearly turned her muscles into jelly. "I know I've said this before, but you've been a godsend, Dillon. Thank you so much for everything that you've been doing."

A compassionate smile pulled at his lips and his gaze softened. "It's no problem."

A few minutes later, they were back in his Jeep and heading down the road. Part of Erin felt like they'd been doing this together forever.

But it had only been a day since Dillon had rescued her from the cliff. Since then, so much had happened. Enough to fill a lifetime it seemed.

She just wanted this to be over with. She wanted to find Bella and try to sleep at night.

Being a single parent wasn't an easy task, but it was worth it. She would make whatever sacrifices necessary for Bella. But the past couple of years hadn't been a cakewalk, especially with Liam's disappearance and the cloud of doubt that had been hanging over Erin since then.

A few minutes later, they pulled up to Grayson Davis's house.

The place was an old two-story house with broken blue siding, a busted window, and piles of junk lining the porch and yard. It wasn't the nicest-looking place, not that it mattered to Erin. But she was glad Dillon was with her in case things turned ugly. She didn't know much about this family, but from the brief snippets she'd heard, the Davises could get rowdy.

Dillon glanced at her before offering an affirmative nod. "Let's do this."

They climbed out and Erin hobbled toward the door.

Before they even climbed the porch steps, the front door opened and a man stepped out, holding a shotgun.

"What do you think you're doing here?" he sneered as he stared them down.

Erin sucked in a breath as she observed the man. Probably in his sixties. Salt-and-pepper beard. Dirty button-up shirt. Old jeans. Hair that could use a good wash.

Then her gaze went back to his gun.

Was he planning to pull the trigger on them?

"Burt Davis," Dillon said. "Do you remember me?"

The man remained silent for several seconds until finally his eyes lit. "You were that cop who helped me find my Emmaline when she wandered off."

Burt's wife had dementia and was known to wander. Dillon and Scout had helped track her down when she'd once gone missing. They'd found her on the edge of a nearby lake. She'd been about to take a swim, despite the winter weather. If they hadn't found her when they had, she would have perished in that water.

"That's me."

Erin listened to every word Burt said, surprised at this side of Dillon. Not that he hadn't seemed heroic already. But hearing about him from someone else offered a different perspective—an affirmation.

Her respect for the man continued to grow.

Burt's shoulders softened. "What brings you by now?"

"We were actually hoping that we could talk to your grandson, Grayson," Dillon said.

Burt's eyes narrowed, not with anger but with what appeared to be resignation. "What's my boy done now?"

"Probably nothing," Dillon said. "Did you hear about the girl who went missing?"

He stared at Dillon, wariness in his gaze. "I did hear something about her while I was in town. What about her?"

"We heard Bella and Grayson were friends, and we're hoping he might have some information that will help us find her." Dillon kept his voice level and even.

"Is that right?" Burt stared at Dillon a moment, that skeptical look still in his gaze.

The man remained silent, chewing on something. Maybe bubble gum. Maybe tobacco. She wasn't sure.

But enough time passed that Erin was certain Burt was going to refuse to let them talk to his grandson.

Despair tried to well inside her again. Had all this been for nothing?

Finally, the man nodded and twisted his head behind him. "Grayson! Get down here.

You have someone here who wants to talk to you."

Erin's lungs nearly froze. He was going to let them talk to Grayson!

Thank you, Jesus!

She couldn't wait to hear if Grayson had additional information to offer about Bella. She prayed that was what would happen, and that this lead might be the one that cracked the case in Bella's disappearance wide open.

Dillon sat at the dining room table. Erin sat beside him and Grayson hunched in his seat across from them. Grayson's granddad stood behind him with his arms crossed and his eyes narrowed, almost as if he dared Grayson to say something he didn't approve of.

Mountains of leftover meals and trash littered the table between them. With it was the scent of rot mixed with old socks and recently cooked collard greens.

Dillon stared at the boy.

Grayson Davis was sixteen with blond hair that he kept cut short. His build was stocky enough that he could play football. He had a thin stubble on his chin, and his gaze focused on the table instead of making eye contact with anyone in the room.

"Thanks for meeting with us," Dillon started, keeping his voice pleasant.

There was no need to start this conversation as if they were enemies. As they sat there, Dillon felt Erin's nerves in her quick movements and shallow breaths.

Thankfully, she was letting him take the lead right now. They didn't want to spook the boy and make him go silent.

"What's going on?" Grayson swallowed hard, his eyes shifting from Dillon to Erin then back to Dillon again.

"We understand that you are friends with Bella Lansing," Dillon said.

Grayson rubbed his hands on his jeans and nodded. "Yeah, we talk."

"When was the last time you talked to her?"

Grayson ran a hand through his hair. "I'm not sure. Maybe two days ago."

Dillon watched the boy carefully, looking for any signs of deceit. "You are aware that she's missing, right?"

Grayson nodded. "I know. I heard. I keep hoping to hear that she has been found."

"Why haven't you come forward to the police yet if the two of you were friends?"

Grayson sighed. "I don't know. I guess because I didn't have anything to tell them. I didn't have anything to offer. Plus, with my family's reputation, I was afraid that they would look at me as a suspect."

"You care about Bella, don't you?" Erin's voice sounded calm and soothing.

Grayson stared at her for a moment before nodding. "Yeah, I do. But she knew you wouldn't approve."

Erin sucked in a breath, his words seeming to shock her. "Is that what she told you?"

"She said that she's not allowed to date. But the two of us really like each other."

"Did she tell you anything that might have indicated that she was in danger?" Dillon asked.

Grayson shifted again, rubbing his hands across his jeans as if he were nervous.

He definitely knew something. The trick would be getting him to share.

"I don't know."

Dillon leaned toward him, clearly about to drive home a point. "Grayson, if there's anything you know, it's important you tell us. We need to find her, and you may know something that will help us do that. You're not in trouble. We are just looking for information."

Grayson remained quiet but sweat had beaded across his forehead.

"You can trust him," Burt said. "Dillon is one of the good guys."

Grayson looked at his granddad and nodded, his eyes still darting all over the place as if he were nervous.

Finally, he looked back at Dillon and Erin. "The day before she went missing, Bella told me she felt like she was being watched."

Erin sucked in a breath beside him. "What else did she say?"

Grayson shrugged. "Not much. She tried to laugh it off and say she was being paranoid. She talked about how much people in this town hated you guys. I think she assumed it was probably just somebody from Liam's side of the family."

Dillon made a note of the fact that Grayson had said Liam instead of her dad. How exactly did Bella view Liam Lansing? He'd ask Erin later.

"No one approached her or did anything?" Dillon continued to press. "Was it just a feeling or was there any action to justify it?"

Grayson rubbed his throat again. "She said she felt someone watching her a couple of times, but she never saw anyone nearby. If anything else happened, Bella didn't tell me."

"Do the two of you text or email each other?" Erin asked.

Grayson nodded, his eyes misting. "I've been trying to talk to her since she left for school two days ago. But I haven't heard back. That's when I knew something was wrong."

Grayson's voice cracked and he wiped beneath his eyes.

He was fighting tears, wasn't he? He really cared about Bella. That was obvious.

Dillon nodded and glanced at Erin. "Anything else?"

Erin shook her head, her eyes lined with grief. "No, but thank you for sharing what you did, Grayson. I'm glad that my daughter has a friend like you."

Relief seemed to fill his gaze at Erin's approval. "I'll let you know if I hear anything else."

As they started toward the door, Burt joined them.

He leaned close to Erin and whispered, "If I were you, I would have killed Liam, too."

Erin froze and glanced at the man, alarm racing through her gaze. "I didn't kill him."

His expression remained unapologetic. "I wouldn't blame you if you did. I had a couple of encounters with him. That man thought he was above the law."

"Yes, he did." Erin's words sounded stiff, as if she were hesitant to agree.

"But if you didn't kill him, then my bets are on the Bradshaws." Burt nodded as if confident of his statement.

Dillon's mind raced. The Bradshaws were a deeply networked family in this area who had drug connections. Dillon suspected they grew pot and sold it, but police were still trying to prove it. Basically, they were trouble, and everyone in these parts knew it.

Dillon put his hand on Erin's arm. He had to get her out of here. Not only did they need to process everything they'd just learned, he could tell she was uncomfortable with where this conversation was going.

"Thank you again for your help," he told Burt and Grayson.

But just as they stepped out the door, a truck drove past. The passenger leaned out the window, his baseball cap pulled down low.

As they watched, the man tossed something from the window.

The next instant, the front yard exploded in flames.

THIRTEEN

"Get down!" Dillon yelled.

The next thing Erin knew, he threw her on the ground and his body covered hers.

An explosion sounded in the front yard before flames filled the air along with the scent of smoke.

Erin's mind could hardly keep up. What had just happened?

She lifted her head and saw fire spreading across the grass in the front yard. She heard a truck squealing away.

The flames appeared to be contained to a small patch of grass. Leftover snow had prevented the fire from spreading.

That was good news.

But it could have turned out a lot differently if she and Dillon had taken just a few steps into the yard.

Dillon rolled off her and also glanced back. "Is everyone okay?"

Burt and Grayson nodded, still looking like they were in shock as they stood inside the doorway.

"What just happened?" Erin muttered.

Dillon rose to his feet before reaching down and helping Erin stand. She brushed imaginary dust from her jeans, mostly so she could forget the tingling feeling she'd felt when her hand touched Dillon's.

She especially didn't trust any tingly feelings or mini firework explosions.

But something about Dillon felt different. Still, she'd be wise to remind herself to keep her distance right now.

"My guess is that it was a bottle bomb." As Dillon scowled at the scene outside, he pulled his phone out and called the police.

"Do you really feel like they'll do anything?" she asked after he ended his call.

"It's hard to say. But we do need to report it." He knew what she was thinking: that the police here weren't reliable anyway.

"Did anybody recognize that truck?" Erin

glanced around the room, but everybody shook their head.

"At least I got a partial of the plates," Dillon said. "But everything happened so fast that I wasn't able to memorize the whole thing."

She shook her head and shivered as the explosion replayed in her mind.

Who would be behind this? The same person who took Bella?

Again, nothing made sense. This whole thing was a nightmare she couldn't seem to wake up from.

She glanced at the front yard again and saw that the flames were gone, leaving smoke, a wide black circle in the lawn, and a few scraps from the bomb itself.

If Erin had to guess, the person who'd done this probably hadn't wanted to kill them. They'd simply wanted to send a message.

What was that message? Was it that Erin wasn't welcome here in Boone's Hollow? That they still thought she'd had something to do with one of these crimes?

It was hard to say. A bad feeling lingered in her gut.

The feeling only worsened when she saw Chief Blackstone pull up several minutes later.

Would he still give her a hard time? Would he ever be on her side, be someone she felt as if she could trust?

She had no idea.

But it was going to take all of her energy and mental strength to get through this next conversation.

"I'll run the plates and see if we get any hits." Chief Blackstone glanced in the distance at Burt before looking back at Dillon.

They all stood in the driveway outside. Three police cars had arrived on scene, and the other officers were collecting evidence and questioning people.

"What are you guys doing here anyway?" Chief Blackstone asked.

"Can't we just pay a friendly visit to some of the town folk?" Dillon didn't want to give this man any more details than he had to.

For some reason, he'd never really liked Blackstone, but his respect had been decreasing steadily ever since this investigation into Bella's disappearance started.

"It's just that you all don't seem like the type who'd hang out with each other." The chief spoke slowly, as if he were purposefully choosing each word. "Unless maybe you're conspiring together."

Dillon felt irritation prickle his skin. "Chief, respectfully, you know that Erin had nothing to do with Bella's disappearance. When you look at all the pieces of the puzzle, it doesn't make sense that she'd do something like this. Besides, how would you explain all the threats that have been made toward her if that was the case?"

Blackstone shrugged. "I like to look at every angle. Maybe she set this up so she wouldn't look guilty."

"What possible reason could she have for wanting to make her daughter disappear?" He didn't bother to keep the exasperation from his voice.

"That's an excellent question. But I heard her girl was giving her a hard time lately. Someone who killed her own husband might be willing and able to do the same to her daughter, too."

Dillon felt Erin tense beside him. Her up-tight body language and quick breathing clearly indicated she could pounce at any minute. He didn't want to put her in a position that would only make her look more guilty.

He gently touched her arm, silently encouraging her to remain quiet.

He understood her anger. He was angry also.

"You know that doesn't make sense." Dillon kept his voice even and diplomatic—for the time being, at least. "I know Liam was your friend and that you need to figure out what happened to him. But you need to expand your pool of suspects outside of Erin."

Blackstone narrowed his eyes and pressed his lips together, not bothering to hide his aggravation. "It sounds like she's got you under her thumb."

"I'm just looking at the evidence. Objectively. That's what you should be doing, too."

Chief Blackstone scowled and took a step

back. "You best watch your tone if you want to get any more jobs around here."

Dillon heard the underlying threat in the man's voice, but Dillon wasn't one to be deterred. His sense of right and wrong was stronger than any threats that could be made against him.

Dillon crossed his arms, unfazed by the chief—and determined to let the man know that. "By the way, any updates on that body that we found in the woods?"

"Not yet," the chief said. "It's still with the medical examiner. In the meantime, we'll look into what happened here tonight. But, based on the lack of evidence, I doubt we're going to figure out who threw this bomb. It was probably just some kids trying to play an innocent prank."

"Bombs are never an innocent prank." Dillon's voice hardened.

"Then maybe this isn't about you guys. Maybe this is about those two." Blackstone nodded toward Burt and Grayson as they stood near the garage and listened. "They like to hang out with unsavory types."

"You don't know what you're talking about,"

Burt called, his gaze daring the chief to defy him.

Dillon turned back to the chief, not liking how this conversation had gone. "Chief Blackstone, I'd appreciate you looking into this matter and taking it seriously."

The man's eyes narrowed. "Need I remind you that I don't take orders from you?"

"Don't be that guy, Chief Blackstone."

The chief stared at Dillon a moment before frowning and walking back to his car.

Dillon hoped that he had laid enough pressure on him that the chief might think twice about how he proceeded. But given the chief's nature, that wasn't a sure thing.

Erin stared out the window, replaying everything that had happened, starting with that conversation with Chief Blackstone.

How could the man be so rude? Such a jerk? And how had he gotten away with it for so long?

She believed in cops. Believed that they did good work. She hated the fact that a couple of bad ones could make all cops look bad, even when that wasn't the case.

But once certain people got into positions of power, like Blackstone had, it felt nearly impossible to change that. To oust them from their positions. And because that was the case, the power trips just seem to keep growing.

Chief Blackstone's was the biggest one of all right now.

"Listen, I know you don't know me that well," Dillon started beside her. "I don't want this to sound weird. But I don't think you should stay at your place by yourself tonight."

Erin froze at Dillon's words. She knew exactly what he was getting at.

Her place wasn't safe.

She wasn't safe.

Erin didn't want to stay by herself, either. But short of leaving town to go stay with family, she didn't have many options. There was no way she would leave this area with Bella still missing.

Dillon had stayed on her couch last night, but she couldn't ask him to do that again. It was too much.

"I'm sure I'll be fine." She didn't sound convincing, even to her own ears.

"How would you feel about sleeping in the spare bedroom at my place? Carson and I will be there, along with all the dogs, of course. You'd have your own space and most people wouldn't even know that you're staying out there."

He raised a good point. Everybody would assume she was staying at her place. Maybe that would allow her to get some rest so she could start fresh the next morning.

"Are you sure you really don't mind? You're going deeper and deeper with me, and I'm afraid that it's going to ruin things for you here in this town."

He ducked his head until they were eye to eye. "Erin, I know it probably feels like everybody here hates you, but I have a hard time believing that's true. Anybody who knows you can clearly see you have a good heart. That you're a good person. Just because a few people—a few loud people—bad-mouth you, don't think they speak for everyone."

Something about his words caused her cheeks to warm. He sounded so sincere, so much like he was speaking the truth. She hadn't expected to crave hearing an affirmation like that. His words brought a strange sense of comfort to her.

"Thank you." Her throat burned as the words left her lips. "I really appreciate that. If you don't mind, I think I will take you up on your offer. I'd feel better if I wasn't at that house by myself tonight."

"Let me just run you past your place so you can pick up a couple of things then."

A few minutes later, she'd packed a small overnight bag and was back in the Jeep with Dillon and Scout. They headed back to his place, another day coming to an end.

Another day without Bella.

Erin continued to pray that her daughter was safe and unharmed. But every day, her prayers felt more and more frail, like she was losing hope that her requests would actually be answered in the way she wanted.

She didn't want to lose faith.

But it was becoming more and more of a struggle.

FOURTEEN

Dillon got Erin settled in the spare bedroom at his house before returning to the living area and starting on some dinner.

He was famished. He'd grabbed a quick sandwich while at the hospital earlier. But certainly Erin was hungry also. Today's events had made him build up an appetite.

He didn't have much to eat, but he could throw together some chicken-and-potato stew. It was one of his go-to staples, and it sounded especially good on such a cold day.

Erin emerged from her room a few minutes later with her hair wet and wearing fresh clothes.

He had to drag his gaze away from her.

He hadn't expected that reaction.

He'd known from the moment he'd met Erin that she was an attractive woman. A very attractive woman. The more he'd gotten to know her, the more he'd been impressed with her character as well.

He'd meant what he had told her earlier. Anybody who had the privilege of actually getting to know Erin had to know she couldn't be responsible for the events that had happened. It was a shame she'd been painted in such a negative light.

He continued to stir his stew as she sat across from him at the breakfast bar. "Dinner?"

"I figured that we both needed to eat," Dillon said. "Carson, too."

She pushed a wet strand of hair behind her ear.

"Thank you for everything you've done." Her voice sounded raw—but sincere—as she said the words.

"I'm just sorry I haven't been able to do more. I want to find Bella also." He bit down, meaning what he'd said. He wasn't going to feel any peace until they had some answers.

"Where do you even think she is right now?" Erin asked. "Do you think she's in the woods? Or did she simply start in the woods? Did she go there to meet somebody who ended up snatching her? If that's the case, where did this person take her?"

"I wish I had those answers for you. But I do know that people have cabins out in those woods where they can live off the land and never be seen. When I was a cop, we assisted park rangers with a search and rescue mission when this woman thought her husband had disappeared. Turned out that instead of divorcing her, he'd run away. He'd lived off-grid for three years before anyone ever found him."

"Wow," Erin muttered. "What did you think when Burt said that the Bradshaws could be responsible? Are you familiar with them?"

"I've heard of them. A lot of people suspect they have a drug enterprise going on in their home. But without any evidence, the police haven't been able to act."

"I see."

Dillon cast another glance at her. "Did you ever suspect that your husband got himself too deeply into a case and disappeared because somebody wanted to silence him or exact revenge?"

"I've tried to think of every angle. But the circumstances of it all were just strange— as was the timing. Especially considering it happened right after a huge fight we had out in public."

"Who initiated the fight?"

"He did. He thought I was seeing someone else, and he told me I shouldn't do that."

"He was the jealous type, huh?"

She frowned and nodded. "To the extreme. We had Officer Hollins over once, and he accused me of flirting with him when I laughed at one of his jokes."

"That doesn't sound healthy."

"It wasn't. All of our fights seemed to go back to him wanting to control me. When things got physical…that's when I knew I had to get out. I couldn't put Bella through that. I couldn't let her see the way he treated me and think that it was okay."

"Leaving him sounds like it was the right thing. I'm sure it also took a certain amount of bravery."

She shrugged. "I don't know about that. But I felt like a burden had been lifted after I'd made the choice. He didn't make it easy on me, unfortunately."

"I can imagine."

Dillon tried to store away every detail just in case it became important later.

He stirred the stew one more time and realized it was close to being done. He was about to grab some bowls when suddenly Scout stood and growled at the front door.

Dillon abandoned his food and pulled his gun out instead.

After everything that had happened, he couldn't take any chances.

"Stay back," Dillon said. "Let me make sure that trouble hasn't found us again."

Erin backed deeper into the kitchen.

Not again.

It just didn't make any sense. Why couldn't this person leave her alone?

She watched as Dillon crept to the window and peered out. Scout stood at his side, on guard and ready to act at the first command.

"Do you see anything?" Her voice trembled as the words left her lips.

"There's a flashlight in the woods," he said.

She sucked in a breath. Somebody really was out there.

Of course.

Scout didn't seem like the type of dog who would react otherwise.

Why would someone be back there? What was this person's plan?

Dillon turned to her, his muscles tight and drawn, as if he were ready to act. The hardness in his eyes surprised her. This whole situation was beginning to get to him as well, wasn't it?

"I'm going to go check it out," he announced.

Alarm raced through her at the thought of him being out there with this person. "Dillon...you could be hurt."

"This needs to end," he said. "Somebody is stalking and threatening you. The situation is bad enough without adding those elements to it."

She couldn't argue with that statement.

But… "I don't want you getting hurt. Too many people have already been hurt."

His determined—and undeterred—gaze met hers. "I'll be careful. I'm going to go out the back door and sneak around the other side of the woods to see if I can take this guy by surprise."

"Do you really think that will work?"

"I don't know, but it's worth giving it a shot." He paused. "Carson!"

A few minutes later, his nephew appeared from upstairs. "Yes?"

"I need you to stay here with Erin and keep an eye on her. You know where the guns are, right?"

Carson stood beside Erin and nodded. "I do. What's going on?"

"Somebody is outside, and I need to figure out who."

Carson stiffened. "Understood. Be safe."

"Always." Dillon nodded at Erin, giving her some type of silent reassurance that everything would be okay.

She wished she felt as confident. But she didn't. Not with so much on the line right now.

Carson went to the closet and opened a safe inside. He pulled out a gun and paced toward the window. He remained there, watching everything outside.

"Do you still see somebody out there?" Erin asked.

He didn't answer for a moment as he stared outside. "Yes, somebody with a flashlight is out there. I can see them moving."

She rubbed her throat, fighting worst-case scenarios.

"My uncle knows these woods better than anybody." Carson seemed to sense her anxiety, to read her mind. "He was a good cop. Competent. He won't put himself in unnecessary danger."

Erin closed her eyes and began lifting prayers. She hoped that Carson was right.

Because her feelings for the man had apparently grown much more quickly than she had ever imagined possible.

Dillon moved carefully through the woods. He couldn't risk giving away his presence.

Not if he wanted to take this person by surprise.

And that was exactly what he wanted to do.

He'd meant what he'd said inside. It was time to put an end to this. This trauma had gone on for far too long.

Besides, if the person in the woods was the same person who'd taken Bella, then Dillon needed to sit him down and demand answers.

None of this made sense to him. None of these games.

Now it was time to find some answers.

He slipped between the trees, watching his every step. If he stepped on one twig wrong, it could mess up everything.

He quietly walked through the woods at the back of the property, skirting the edge of those woods and carefully remaining out of sight.

The person he'd spotted had been lurking near the front of his property. The flashlight Dillon had seen had indicated movement.

Was this person looking for a good vantage point to spy on Erin? Or was the reason someone was out here even more deadly? Perhaps the intruder was searching for the best position to pull the trigger.

Anger burned through Dillon's blood at the thought.

Erin didn't deserve to go through this. If Dillon could do anything to stop it, he would. It was the same reason that he was determined to leave in the morning and to begin search efforts for Bella again. If the girl was out in the Pisgah National Forest, Dillon wanted to find her.

He gripped his gun, his muscles tense as he wondered exactly how this would play out. Though he'd given up being a cop, another part of him would always be a cop. Would always want to look out for people who needed help. To be a voice for the voiceless.

He continued forward, snow crunching beneath his boots. As the temperature dropped, everything was becoming icy again. The threadbare trees didn't allow much cover. But he was deep enough in the forest that he could maintain his distance.

He rounded the curve of the trees, headed

toward the front of the house where he had seen the light.

As he did, he paused.

Where had the trespasser gone? Enough time had passed that the person could have walked deeper into the woods or closer to the driveway. Dillon couldn't afford to walk into a situation not knowing what was happening around him.

He held his breath as he waited, watching for that flashlight he'd spotted earlier. Listening for any telltale footsteps.

If he'd wanted to risk it, he could have turned on his own flashlight and shone it on the ground to search for any footprints. But that was a risk he couldn't afford to take. He couldn't give away his presence.

He continued to wait and listen.

Still nothing.

As he waited, he wondered how the person had even gotten here without his noticing a vehicle.

If he had to guess, the intruder had probably parked on the side of the road and then cut through the woods.

Dillon would check that out later, if necessary.

For now, maybe the man had moved farther away.

Dillon crept forward a few more steps, trying to find a different vantage point.

But as he did, a stick cracked behind him.

The next thing he knew, something hard came down over his head and everything began to spin.

FIFTEEN

Erin stood at the window and stared out the crack between the curtain and the wall. She knew that Dillon wouldn't want her standing that close. Especially if bullets were to start to fly again.

Whoever was behind these threats was certainly persistent. In fact, he was relentless.

Could it be Liam? If so, where had he been hiding out the past year?

But when she remembered the body they'd found with his necklace on it, she knew that wasn't the case. That had to be Liam, right? Who else would it be?

Could Liam's family be behind everything that was happening? Or had Liam made someone mad and now this person was trying to get revenge on Liam's family as some type of ultimate payback?

Erin had no idea, but she didn't like any of this.

"Are you doing okay?" Carson stood on the other side of the window, gun in hand.

She shrugged. "I guess as well as can be expected."

"It sounds like you've gone through a lot."

"It feels like I've gone through a lot."

Carson glanced outside again before saying, "Dillon used to be one of the best cops out there, you know?"

"Is that right?" Erin really wanted to ask what happened, but she figured it wasn't her business. Maybe, if she were lucky, Dillon would tell her later.

"It seems like every cop has that one case that gets to him," Carson said, still keeping an eye on the window. "My uncle went to find a missing hiker. His team searched everywhere but didn't find him. A day after they called off the search, the man's body was discovered within a half-mile radius of where my uncle searched. He's beat himself up over it ever since."

Erin soaked in each new detail, a better picture of Dillon forming in her head. "Certainly it wasn't his fault. He seems very thorough."

"He would have probably realized that eventually," Carson said. "But the family of the hiker who died began to attack my uncle. They sued the police department, and Dillon became the poster child of botched rescue operations. He was the face that they put with their grievances."

She let out a small gasp. "That couldn't have been easy."

"It wasn't. He was engaged at the time, but his fiancée couldn't handle the pressure. She broke things off with him. Talk about a hard time."

Erin shook her head, unable to understand how somebody could leave someone they loved in the midst of turmoil. "I can only imagine how difficult that had to be for him."

Carson kept one eye on the front yard as he talked. "It definitely changed him. But I truly believe he's doing what he loves right now. He's really good with dogs and training them. Plus, I think that in some way it helps him to feel like he can make amends for the mistakes that he blames himself for."

The new insight into Dillon painted him in a different light.

In some ways, Erin could understand exactly where he was coming from. She had lived under the weight of accusation. It wasn't a fun place to be, and people rarely came out the same on the other side.

"If you don't mind me asking, how long have you lived with your uncle?"

"Two years," he said. "He's not really my uncle, but he's my father's best friend. My mom left us when I was thirteen and my dad started drinking pretty heavily. He needed help. Uncle Dillon paid to send him to rehab. He's still trying to get his life back together, to be honest. Uncle Dillon said I could stay here for as long as necessary."

"I'm sorry to hear about all that, but I'm glad you have someone like Dillon in your life." Again, her perspective on Dillon changed— in a good way.

He was a good man. It wasn't just a mask he wore around her.

Her admiration for the man grew.

Erin's gaze went back to the window, and she wondered what was happening outside. She was going to give Dillon five more minutes. Then she would push past Carson and go check on Dillon herself.

What if something was wrong? What if he needed them?

He had done so much for her. There was no way Erin was going to leave him in his time of need, especially since she was the source of all this trouble.

She crossed her arms over her chest and waited.

Five minutes.

That was all.

Then she was going to have to take action.

Just as Dillon felt everything spinning around him, a shock of adrenaline burst through him and he sprang into action.

He swirled around and saw a man in a black mask standing in front of him with a shovel in his hands.

He braced himself for a fight before muttering, "I don't think so."

As the man swung the shovel at him again, Dillon ducked. His shoulder caught the masked man in the gut, and they crashed to the ground.

As another wave of nausea rushed over Dillon, the man flipped him over. The guy's fist collided with Dillon's jaw, and pain rippled through him.

But Dillon still had more fight in him left. This was far from over.

He grabbed the guy and shoved him backward. Dillon's hand went to the man's throat as he pinned the intruder to the ground.

The man grunted and thrashed beneath him. Whoever he was, he was strong, and Dillon had to use all in his energy to keep the man pinned.

If only Dillon could see who was on the other side of that mask. But if he shifted his weight to pull it off, he feared the guy would take advantage of his disheveled state and get the upper hand.

"Where is Bella?" Dillon demanded.

The trespasser grunted.

In one motion, the man shoved Dillon off and burst to his feet.

Dillon stood just in time.

With his hands in front of him, the man rammed Dillon into the tree.

His head spun.

Dillon straightened to go after the man again, but before he could, the man took off in a run.

Dillon staggered forward, still not ready to give up. But as everything swirled around him, he realized he wasn't going to make it if he chased this guy.

That blow to his head was making him light-headed and nauseous.

He started to take one more step forward just out of stubborn determination.

As he did, he crumpled to the ground.

He'd been so close to finding answers. So close.

But he'd let the man get away.

"I'm going out there." Erin stepped toward the door.

Carson moved in front of her, blocking her

path. "I can't let you do that. I promised my uncle that I wouldn't."

"He might need our help."

"He can handle himself." Carson's voice contained full confidence in his words.

"He's been out there too long. What if he's hurt?" Her voice trembled with emotion. She was honestly worried about Dillon.

Something flashed in Carson's gaze. Was that fear? The realization that she might be right?

"You stay in here." Carson's voice hardened with surprising maturity. "I'll check."

"I'm going with you," Erin insisted. "There's no way I'm letting a teenager go out there and get hurt on my account."

He stared at her a moment before marching to the closet. He pulled out another gun and handed it to her. "Do you know how to handle one of these?"

She stared at the small handgun and nodded, her throat suddenly feeling dry. "I do."

"Good. Bring it with you. It's fully loaded. Use it if you need to."

A shiver of apprehension raced down her

spine. Erin really prayed that she didn't have to use this. But if it came down to Dillon's life or someone else's?

She knew that she had to protect these people who had protected her. She would aim for a shoulder or a knee or something nonlethal. She could do this.

As she walked with Carson toward the back door, another surge of apprehension rippled up her spine. She really had no idea what she was doing right now. She only knew she had to help Dillon.

"We're going to skirt around the backside of the property, just like my uncle did," Carson said. "We don't want to make ourselves easy targets for this guy if he's still out there."

Erin nodded and gripped the gun in both hands.

With one more nod from Carson, they both stepped outside into the dark, tranquil night. She scanned everything around her, looking for a sign of anything that might have happened. Dark woods stared back at her, looking deceitfully peaceful with the white snow covering the branches and ground.

Everything seemed still and quiet.

Carson motioned for her to follow, and they took off in a run toward the trees. Once they reached the cover of the woods, they followed a small path around the edge of the property.

The temperature had dipped close to zero, and it felt every bit like it. Snow crunched beneath her feet no matter how hard she tried to stay quiet. Her nose already felt numb, as did her fingers.

But those were the least of her concerns. Dillon was her main focus right now.

As they neared the area where they'd seen the flashlight, Carson put a finger over his lips, motioning for her to be quiet. They slowed their steps as they crept forward.

Erin kept her gaze on everything around her, looking for any signs of trouble.

She saw nothing. No one. No lights. Nor did she hear anything.

Exactly what had gone on out here?

What if that man had grabbed Dillon just like someone had grabbed Bella?

A sick feeling gurgled in Erin's gut at the thought of it.

She continued forward and, with every step, the tension in her back muscles only increased.

Erin had hoped they would have found Dillon by now. That he would have offered an explanation for what was taking so long and then ushered them back into the warmth and safety of the house, giving them a good lecture in the process.

But that wasn't the case.

Her thoughts on Dillon, Erin nearly collided into Carson's back. He let out a breath in front of her, and that's when she knew that something was wrong.

She peered around him and spotted Dillon on the ground.

Not moving.

Alarm raced through her. Was he dead? *Oh, God. Please...no!*

Dillon startled when he heard a noise above him. But as he tried to sit up, pain shot through his skull.

At once, everything rushed back to him.

The intruder in the woods. The one who'd

hit him with a shovel. Who'd pushed him into the tree. Had ultimately gotten away.

Or had he?

Dillon felt the shadow over him and raised his fists, ready to fight.

"Wait! It's just us, Dillon."

Slowly, Carson's face came into view. Erin stood beside him, worry in her gaze as she looked down at him.

Dillon scowled as he rubbed the back of his head. "What are you guys doing out here? I told you to stay inside."

"We came to check on you," Carson said. "It looks like it's a good thing we did."

He rubbed the back of his head again, wishing that it didn't hurt as badly as it did. There was no way he could pretend that he wasn't in pain. No way that he could pretend nothing had happened out here.

Carson took one of his arms and Erin the other as they helped him to his feet.

"Where's the person who did this to you?" Carson demanded, his gaze hardening with anger.

"He got away. I tried to catch him, but we ended up in a fistfight."

"You obviously hurt your head." Erin stared at him, worry still lingering in her gaze.

"I'm fine." He brushed her concern off with the shake of his head.

"You don't look fine." Erin wrapped her hand around his arm so she wouldn't lose her grip. "We need to get you inside and check your head for injuries."

Dillon knew better than to argue at this point. Besides, his head pounded with every new line of conversation. The sooner he could get this over with, the better.

He dropped an arm over both of their shoulders, and they helped him through the woods and back into the house. Scout greeted him with a wet nose as soon as he stepped inside, letting out a little whine to let him know he'd been worried also.

He rubbed the dog's head before sitting on the couch. Erin hurried across the room and grabbed a glass of water, handing it to him and insisting he take a drink.

He complied.

Even as he did, all he could think about was that man. Dillon had been so close to catching him, to finding answers.

Just like he had been so close to finding Michael Masterson.

Guilt seemed to dogpile on top of his regret and he squeezed his eyes shut.

"Let me see the back of your head," Erin said. "Carson, can you get him some ice for his face?"

Carson hurried into the kitchen.

As he did, Erin moved to the back of the couch and leaned over him. "I don't see any cuts. But you might have a concussion. We should take you to the hospital."

He started to shake his head when everything wobbled around him again. "I'll be fine."

"I think she's right." Carson returned and handed an ice pack wrapped in a dishtowel to his uncle. "It couldn't hurt to be checked out."

"I'm telling you, I'm fine. I'm going to have a headache, and I need to watch myself when I go to sleep tonight but, otherwise, I'm going to be okay." He pressed the compress against his cheek.

He didn't miss the look that Erin and Carson exchanged with each other. They were both worried about him. He supposed he should be grateful he had people in his life to worry over him. Some people didn't have that privilege.

"How about some coffee?" Erin asked. "Would that make anything better?"

"That sounds great." The caffeine would help him stay awake, which he knew was important right now. Plus, he needed some space.

A few minutes later, she brought him a cup before lowering herself beside him on the couch. Her wide-eyed gaze searched his. "What happened out there?"

As tonight's events filled his thoughts, he closed his eyes, wishing he could have a replay. But that wasn't always possible in life.

Instead, he sighed before starting. "The guy must have heard me coming. He hit me in the back of the head with a shovel. I thought I was coming out ahead until he pushed me into a tree. Everything went black around me. The last thing I remember is him running away."

"Did you get a good look at him?" Erin asked.

Dillon frowned. "Unfortunately, I didn't. He was wearing a black mask, and it was dark outside. I couldn't even tell you his eye color."

"What about his voice?" Carson asked. "Was there anything distinct about it?"

"I already thought about that. I wish I had something to report to you guys. I really do. But there's nothing. I even tried to ask him where Bella was, but he just grunted in response."

"If he wasn't involved in this, then he would have denied it, right?" Erin's voice contained a touch of fear that mingled with hope.

"I definitely think he has something to do with what's going on. I don't know if he's the person who grabbed Bella or not. But this is all connected. We just need to figure out how."

Erin's hand went over her mouth as she squeezed her eyes shut. "I shouldn't be here. I'm putting you in danger."

The thought of her leaving and being on her own right now caused a strange grief to grip his heart.

"I don't want you to leave." The surprisingly raw and honest words surprised even him. And Erin, too. Clearly, because her eyes widened. "I'd just feel better if you were here where we can keep an eye on you."

"But if these attacks continue and you're constantly in the line of fire..."

His gaze locked with hers. "I'm in the line of fire because I put myself there. You leaving won't take me out of that position now. Do you understand?"

She stared at him another moment, and Dillon wasn't sure what she was going to say. Part of him thought that she might just up and leave.

He held his breath as he waited to see what her response would be.

SIXTEEN

If Erin were smart, she'd leave. If she really cared about Dillon, Carson and Scout as much as she thought she did, she'd get out of here before any more damage could be done.

But as she stared at Dillon now and saw the sincerity in his eyes, everything in her wanted to stay.

She knew it was selfish. She didn't want to do anything that she would regret. But she felt certain that if she went back to her house tonight, things wouldn't end well. The person who was pursuing her wasn't letting up. The only way this would end would be with her dead.

She licked her lips before nodding at Dillon as he sat on the couch, compress still against his face. "If you don't mind, I will stay. But the moment you want me gone, you let me know, and I'm out of here. I'm serious."

Something that looked close to relief flooded Dillon's gaze. "Good. I think you're making a smart decision."

Erin reminded herself that Dillon's reasons for wanting her to stay were purely professional. Nothing about this case was personal. She needed to remember to keep her walls up as well. Just because she felt safe with Dillon didn't mean anything.

Quickly, she stood and went into the kitchen to check on the stew. "Would you like some? I think it's done."

"Maybe some food is just what the doctor ordered."

"You stay there. I'll get it ready." She found some bowls and spoons. A few minutes later, she had the table set for three.

Erin wanted to pretend like this was just a normal dinner with new friends, but she knew it was anything but. They were together right now simply because they wanted to survive.

After praying, they all dug into the warm meal.

Erin took her first bite of the stew and the

flavors of nutmeg and garlic washed over her taste buds. "This is delicious."

She hadn't known what to expect.

"It's my mom's recipe," Dillon said. "She's quite the cook—and comfort food is her specialty."

"Where are you parents now?" she asked.

"They retired down in Florida. I still get to see them several times a year, though."

"That's nice."

"How about you, Erin?" Dillon asked. "Where are you from?"

"I grew up closer to Raleigh, but Liam and I met in college. He was from this area, so we moved here."

"This is God's country," Carson said. "At least, in my eyes that's what it is."

Erin smiled. "No one can deny it's beautiful out here."

They chatted about the area as they finished their meal, and then Erin cleaned up while Dillon moved to the couch, still looking worse for the wear after the confrontation in the woods.

As the dogs began barking outside, Dillon

glanced at Carson. "Would you mind checking on the dogs?"

"No, sir. I'll do that now." Carson grabbed his coat and started toward the back door.

"Be careful out there," Dillon called.

His words were a reminder of the danger they were all currently in.

As he left the room, Erin sat beside Dillon on the couch and felt the tension stretch between them.

Now that her emotions over what happened were settling down, she had to wonder what they were going to talk about. She sucked in a deep breath, deciding to address the unspoken issues they were both certainly thinking about.

She cleared her throat. "Are you sure you don't want to call the police and tell them what happened tonight?"

Dillon's expression tightened. "No, they're not going to do anything. First thing in the morning, I'll go out and investigate for myself."

He really didn't like Blackstone, either.

Why did Erin find so much comfort in that thought?

She pulled her legs beneath her and leaned against the couch as she turned to Dillon. "Have you heard anything about the search and rescue operations for Bella tomorrow?"

"Rick told me they're going to take the helicopter out again and that there will be more search and rescue teams. I'll take Scout out and see if he can pick up her scent again. At least we have a basic idea of what direction Bella traveled in."

Erin nodded, trying not to show her anxiety.

Dillon shifted closer to her before lowering his voice. "Erin, I haven't been in your exact shoes. But I feel like another part of me knows what you're going through."

She stared at him, curious about what he might share. Was this concerning what Carson had told her? About his ex-fiancée who'd left him?

"How so?" she finally asked.

He lowered his compress and put it on the table as a far-off look flooded his eyes. "A lot of people turned against me when one of my search and rescue missions went south. Even my fiancée ended up leaving me because she couldn't take the pressure of it."

"I'm sorry to hear that."

"I deal all the time with people who have missing loved ones. I feel like I live their experiences with them sometimes."

Spontaneously, she reached forward and grabbed his hand. "I can only imagine."

As they looked at each other, their gazes caught.

Their grief had bonded them, hadn't it? They'd both been through ordeals that only the other could understand.

Erin still marveled at the fact that Dillon was so unlike Liam. He was a breath of fresh air—and he brought her a renewed hope.

"Erin?" His voice sounded scratchy as he said the word.

"Yes?" Was she imagining things or was he leaning closer?

The next moment, he reached forward and pushed a lock of hair behind her ear. His gaze almost looked smoky with emotion—and the look in his eyes took her breath away.

It wasn't just attraction there. It was genuine care and concern.

His thumb brushed across her cheek as he moved in closer.

She closed her eyes, anticipating what might happen next.

Until a new sound cut into the moment.

Dillon's phone.

He pulled back, seeming to snap out of the impulsive moment.

Instead, Dillon excused himself and grabbed the device from the table.

Erin tried not to feel disappointed.

It was best that kiss hadn't happened. The interruption was probably a godsend, a reminder that she was better off going solo rather than getting tangled in a bad situation again.

So why did it feel like Dillon would never create a bad scenario in her life?

Dillon saw Rick's number on the screen and his breath caught.

His heart still pounded out of control from

the near kiss. It only accelerated more when he realized his friend might have an update.

He answered and put the call on the speaker. "Rick, I'm here with Erin. She's listening."

"Perfect," Rick said. "I just wanted to let you know that a hiker on a different trail found a shoe that I believe belongs to Bella."

Dillon's breath caught. "What trail?"

"Gulch Valley," Rick said.

Dillon frowned as he pictured the layout of trails in the park. "That's on the other side of the park."

"I know." Rick's voice sounded somber. "It doesn't make any sense."

Dillon shook his head as he tried to think through this newest update. "Scout couldn't have been that wrong. Bella was definitely in the part of the forest that we searched."

"I agree. But how did her shoe end up nearly twenty miles away?"

Dillon bit down as he imagined various scenarios. None of his theories rose to the surface, however. "That's a good question."

"It's a possibility that someone took her

shoe and left it as a means of misdirection," Rick said.

"Do you think somebody would do that?" Erin's voice sounded wispy with surprise.

"It's hard to say for sure," Rick said. "We've involved several other local police departments in our search, including the guys from Boone's Hollow. Chief Blackstone said his guys were going to search that area tomorrow as well and see if they could pick up on anything."

"I'm glad he's doing something," Dillon muttered.

They ended the call with a promise to keep each other updated.

Then silence stretched between them.

As the back door opened, Carson wandered inside. "The dogs are fine. I'm not sure why they started barking."

"That's good news, at least." Erin stood and rubbed her hands down the sides of her pants as if she were nervous. "Now that Carson is back, I think I should probably be getting some rest."

Dillon nodded, wondering if something had

spooked her. Had he said something? Or was it just this situation?

"I'm going to get Carson to stay awake with me for a little while," Dillon finally said. "I probably shouldn't go to sleep right now after my head injury."

"That's probably a good idea. Do you need me to—"

Dillon shook his head before Erin could finish the sentence. "I'll be fine."

Erin stared at him a moment, questions lingering in her gaze.

Maybe the two of them needed a little time apart. Their emotions had grown quickly, fueled by the danger around them. The last thing he wanted was to do something in the heat of the moment that they would both later regret.

"Carson and I have got this," Dillon insisted. "You get your sleep."

Erin stared at him a moment longer before nodding. "Okay then. I'll talk to you in the morning."

"I'll see you then."

But as she disappeared down the hallway,

he couldn't help but wonder what kind of trouble tomorrow would hold.

As Erin laid in bed, she couldn't stop thinking about the kiss she'd almost shared with Dillon.

What would it be like to open herself up to somebody again? Part of her felt thrilled at the possibility and another part of her only felt fear.

Liam had been the only guy she'd ever dated, and she hadn't dated anyone since he'd disappeared. She'd had no desire to.

But something about Dillon was different. He was gentle. Respectful.

Then again, Liam had been those things at first also. People said you never really knew a person until you went through the hard times with them. That was when their true colors seemed to appear.

Erin had to agree with those words.

She frowned at the memories.

It was a good thing that the kiss had been interrupted. Erin needed to slow down. They both did. Their emotions were clearly out of control.

But another part of her felt like there could be something special there between her and Dillon.

As she punched her pillow, trying to get comfortable, she tried to put any thoughts of Dillon out of her mind. The only person she needed to think about right now was Bella. To engage in any type of romance while her daughter was missing would be uncouth.

That was right.

Until Bella was found, romance was totally off the table, even with someone like Dillon.

Besides, who knew what was going to happen once this was all over. What if Bella wasn't found? Just like Liam hadn't been found.

Or Bella might need help after she was rescued. Erin's life might be devoted to counseling sessions as she tried to help Bella deal with the aftermath of this ordeal. That *had* to be Erin's first priority.

As she turned over in bed again, a noise in the corner of the room caught her ear.

She froze.

What was that?

Sometimes, new houses had different sounds, she reminded herself. Had the heat kicked on? Had a branch scraped the window?

Erin listened, desperate to hear the sound again so she could confirm the noise was mundane and nothing to be worried about.

All was quiet.

She waited a few more seconds, trying to write off the sound. Maybe sleep would find her. Maybe her brain would turn off. Maybe she could stop worrying so much over something so trivial.

Liam had always said Erin liked to make big deals out of nothing.

He'd used the word *trivial* quite a bit. Now, even the thought of that word made Erin's insides tighten as bad memories began to pummel her.

She turned over, determined to get some rest.

But just as she did that, the noise filled the room again.

The next instant, somebody pounced on top of her and a hand covered her mouth.

SEVENTEEN

Erin felt tension pulsing through her as the intruder pinned her down.

She froze, unable to move, unable to defend herself. All she wanted to do was panic.

Who was in her room? How did he get in here?

Even worse: what was he planning?

"You're not going to get away with this," a deep voice muttered in her ear. "Do you understand me?"

Erin remained frozen, unable to react or respond. Her heart thudded in her ears at a rapid pace.

"I said, do you understand me?" he repeated, his voice a growl.

Erin forced herself to nod. The man's hand clutching her mouth made it impossible to speak.

"You deserve to suffer," he continued. "You deserve everything you've got coming for you."

Her blood went cold. Why was this man doing this?

He didn't seem interested in hurting her—only in making her suffer.

But why?

Did this go back to Liam?

"Don't make me tell you again. And yes, I have more in store for you. Ending it like this would be too easy."

What was this guy talking about?

Maybe Erin didn't want to know.

"I'm going to slip out of your room," the man continued. "If you make a sound, I will kill Bella. Do you understand me?"

Kill Bella? *This* was the man who'd taken her? Why had he broken into Dillon's house? Just to threaten her like this?

Her chill deepened.

"I said, do you understand?" His rancid breath hit her ear.

Erin nodded again, more quickly this time.

"Good, because I'm going to be watching. One wrong move and she's dead."

A cry caught in Erin's throat at the thought. The next instant, the weight of the man's body lifted from her.

Erin pulled in a deep breath, relishing the gulp of air as it filled her lungs.

In a flash, the man opened a window and rushed out.

A cool wind swept through the room.

Otherwise, everything was quiet.

Erin waited, her pounding heart the only sound she heard.

Had that really just happened? It still seemed like a nightmare.

She waited several minutes and tried to compose herself. She knew she needed to move. But she couldn't seem to force her body into action.

Get up, Erin. You're wasting time. Push through the fear!

Finally, she threw her legs out of bed. Her limbs trembled as adrenaline claimed her muscles.

She rose to her feet and peered out the window.

But the man was gone.

Erin had to get Dillon. Had to tell him what had just happened.

She only hoped she could make it out of this room in time.

Dillon straightened from his position on the couch as he heard footsteps rushing down the hallway. Carson sat in the chair across from him, so that had to be Erin.

Was she having trouble sleeping?

When he saw the expression on her face, he knew something was wrong.

He rose, worry pulling taut across his back muscles. "Erin?"

"A man…was in…my room." She clung to the wall as her red-rimmed eyes stared at him.

Even from across the room, Dillon could see her shaking.

He darted toward her and slipped an arm around her waist. He led her to the couch and lowered her onto the cushions before she collapsed.

"A man was in your room? Here at my house?" Had Dillon heard her correctly?

"He went out the window. He's gone now." Her voice broke as if she fought a moan.

Dillon looked at Carson, who'd also risen to his feet. "Did you see or hear anything?"

"No." He shook his head, his stiff shoulders indicating he was on guard. "Not a single thing."

Dillon turned back to Erin, desperate for more information. "What did he say?"

She drew in a shaky breath. "He said I wasn't going to get away with this, that I deserved to suffer, and that I deserved everything I had coming to me."

Concern pulsed through him. He couldn't believe Scout hadn't picked up on the stranger's scent. But the evening had been hectic. He had noticed the canine whine once, but he'd assumed it was from the chaos around them.

"Anything else?" Dillon asked.

"He said he had more in store for me, and that ending it like this would be too easy. Before he left, he said he would be watching, and if I made one wrong move, Bella would die." Her voice broke as a sob wracked her body.

Dillon put an arm around her shoulders before pulling her to him in a hug.

He didn't say anything for a moment. He just held her, comforted her. Carson set a box of tissues beside them, and Erin grabbed one to wipe her face.

She drew in another breath and seemed to compose herself for a moment. "What am I going to do?"

"That's what we need to figure out," Dillon muttered. "Why would someone go through the trouble of breaking in just to tell you that?" Dillon asked.

"It's like he said—he wants to make me suffer. To let me know that I have no control, yet all of this is my fault." Erin's voice broke as if she held back a cry.

Her words settled on him. They made sense—in a twisted kind of way at least.

"That was why that man was outside the house earlier," Dillon mumbled.

Erin sucked in a quick breath as she stared

up at him. "Do you mean that he drew us outside just so somebody else could sneak inside?"

"That's my best guess. That's the only thing that makes sense."

"But *none* of this makes sense. Why would the person who abducted Bella go through all this trouble?" She pressed the tissue into her eyes again.

The truth slammed into Dillon's mind. How had he not seen this before?

"That's because this isn't about Bella," Dillon muttered. "This is about you, Erin."

Realization spread through Erin's gaze and she nodded. "You're right. This *is* about me. I'm the actual target here, aren't I?"

Dillon almost didn't want to agree with her, but he had no choice. Erin had to know what she was up against.

"What am I going to do, Dillon?" Her wide eyes met his, questions filling their depths.

His heart ached for the woman.

He reached forward and squeezed her hand. "I don't know. But I'll be here with you to help you figure it out."

* * *

Erin startled awake.

Where was she? What was going on?

All she felt was a cold fear that pierced her heart.

Danger seemed to hang in the air around her.

"It's okay," a deep voice murmured beside her.

Erin jumped back even farther.

Who was that?

She glanced up and her eyes slowly adjusted to the darkness.

Dillon's face stared back at her.

Erin let out a breath. She must have fallen asleep on the couch. Had her head been on his shoulder?

Her cheeks heated at the thought of it.

The events of last night flooded back to her and she shivered. Especially when she remembered the man who'd been in her room—the person who wanted to strike fear into her heart.

He had succeeded. He'd taken away everything that was precious to her. Erin's sense of security. Her peace of mind. Her faith in humanity.

Most of all—he'd taken away Bella.

She held back a cry.

The only thing the man hadn't taken was her faith in God, but even that felt like it was on shaky ground lately. This situation was definitely a test of her faith.

Dillon shifted beside her before softly murmuring, "I didn't want to wake you."

Erin raked her hand through her hair and nodded. She vaguely remembered Dillon holding her as they'd sat on the couch. She remembered resting her head on his shoulder.

She must have fallen asleep.

She rubbed her throat as she felt another wave of self-consciousness. "I'm sorry… I didn't mean to…"

"No need for apologies." Dillon glanced at her, his eyes warm and almost soft. "I'm glad you were able to get some rest."

She studied his face for a moment, wondering how his concussion was—not to mention his swollen cheek. She wasn't the only one suffering here.

"How about you?" She studied his face. "Do you feel okay?"

"I'm fine."

He shrugged, but Erin knew that meant he hadn't gotten any rest. He was simply trying to play it off, and maybe he was even worried that Erin might feel guilty over all that had happened.

He was always so considerate of her feelings, a fact she deeply appreciated.

"What time is it?" Erin rubbed her eyes again, wishing she didn't feel so groggy.

"Almost 6:00 a.m."

She let out a breath. She must have been out. On a subconscious level, she had realized she was safe with Dillon so close.

Her cheeks heated at the thought.

"I can't believe I slept that long," she murmured.

"You must have needed it."

She couldn't argue with that point. "Have you heard any updates?"

Dillon shook his head. "Unfortunately, no."

Erin pushed herself to her feet, needing a

moment to compose herself. "Would it be okay if I hopped in the shower real quick?"

Dillon's perceptive eyes met hers. "Go right ahead. Maybe that will make you feel better."

She wished something as simple as a shower had that power. But all she wanted right now was Bella.

She needed her daughter.

With every day that passed, her worry only grew.

And there didn't seem to be an end in sight.

She only hoped today might provide some answers.

EIGHTEEN

Dillon instructed Carson to stay inside the house to keep an eye out for trouble. While Carson was on guard, Dillon put his boots and coat on before going outside to search for any evidence of what happened last night.

Just as Erin had told him, footprints came from the window near her bedroom.

Anger zipped through his blood at the thought of what had happened. The person behind this was brazen—a little too brazen for his comfort.

Yet the man hadn't wanted to hurt Erin. He'd only wanted to scare her. To draw out her suffering.

He pulled out his phone and took some pictures of the footprints, using a dollar bill for size. Then he continued following the footprints.

The steps led into the woods. As Dillon crossed into the tree line, memories of being whacked in the head with that shovel filled him. Each thought made his muscles tense.

His head still throbbed, but he felt better today than he had yesterday. He was grateful to be alive. He'd known people who'd lost their lives after taking blows like that.

He continued into the woods, but the footsteps became harder to follow under the brittle canopy of branches above. They'd protected the ground below, preventing snow from reaching it. Without as much snow here, the tracks weren't as obvious.

As Dillon crossed through the small patch of woods to the street on the other side, he spotted tire prints on the edge of the road. Just as he'd expected, someone had pulled of the street, parked there, and then done their dirty deed.

This whole thing didn't make sense to Dillon.

Why go through so much trouble just to teach Erin a lesson? What kind of logic was this person following?

Unless there was something he was missing.
Dillon frowned.

He had to get to the bottom of this and soon.

Dillon headed back to the house. He'd need to change and get ready also so he could meet the rest of the search party. He hoped that maybe they could find some answers today.

Not only for Bella's sake, but for Erin's well-being also.

How many more hits could she take?

He didn't know, but she'd had more than her fill.

Erin glanced up as Dillon stepped back into the room. She quickly flipped a piece of bacon on the griddle.

"I hope you don't mind," she said. "But I figured we could both use our energy today."

"No, not at all. It smells great." He stomped his boots to get the snow off as he closed the door behind him. After hanging his coat on a rack, he strode toward her.

Erin hadn't been sure if she should cook or not. She hadn't wanted to overstep.

She'd taken a quick shower and hadn't bothered to dry her hair. At least she had clean clothes on, and she'd brushed her teeth. Despite her doubts, Erin felt a little more alert than she had earlier.

"Anything new outside?"

When Carson had told her that Dillon had stepped out, Erin had figured he was looking for clues. But as she'd prepared breakfast, she hadn't been able to stop thinking about what Dillon might have discovered.

"I found footprints and tire prints." Dillon paused near her. "I took pictures of them, just in case."

"At least it's something." Erin wasn't sure what else to say. It wasn't exactly like she'd been expecting Dillon to catch the person responsible.

Dillon pulled out a barstool across from the kitchen island cooktop and sat down. "Can I help?"

She shook her head as she flipped another piece of bacon. "I'm fine. You can just take it easy. In fact, if you want to go get ready, our food should be done by the time you change."

He nodded and stood—almost seeming reluctant do so.

As Erin watched him walk away, her throat tightened.

Something about this arrangement felt a little too cozy. Why was Erin letting her emotions get the best of her like this? The rush of attraction she felt for Dillon threw her off balance, especially given everything else that was going on.

"Life can be pretty confusing sometimes, can't it, Scout?" She glanced down at the canine who sat at her feet, probably hoping she'd drop some food on the floor.

He raised his nose in the air and sniffed in response.

Just as she'd predicted, Dillon had finished getting ready just as Erin pulled the eggs off the burner. A few minutes later, they sat across from each other at the small dining room table, Carson joining them. After Dillon prayed, they all dug in.

Erin was especially touched by the prayer he had lifted for Bella.

Be with Bella. Keep her safe as only You

can do, Lord. Wrap Your loving arms around her and give her comfort. Most of all, help us find her.

But as soon as she took her first bite, Dillon turned toward her. The serious look in his gaze indicated that something was wrong.

"Rick called just as I got out of the shower," he started.

She wiped her mouth before leaving her napkin on her lap. "And?"

Dillon's face tightened as if he were having trouble forming his words.

That couldn't be good.

"Bella's other shoe was found," he finally said. "It was located about five hundred feet from the first one."

Erin stared at him, trying to read between the lines. Trying not to jump to worst-case scenarios. Trying to stay positive.

But she had to ask... "Is that a bad sign?"

He pressed his lips together, the ends pulling down in a frown, before he finally said, "There was a small amount of blood on it."

Dillon practically inhaled his breakfast.

There was no time to waste.

As soon as he took his last bite, he stood and turned to his nephew. "Carson, I'm going to need you to utilize all that training we've been working on. You need to take Scout out there in the search for Bella."

Erin's breath caught beside him. "Why wouldn't you go? I hear you're the best."

"You're not going to be able to walk those trails." He nodded at her twisted ankle.

"Then you can go without me," she insisted.

He shook his head, knowing that wasn't going to work out for multiple reasons. "I don't want to leave you alone. Not after everything that has happened. It wouldn't be safe."

"But finding Bella is more important than my safety!" Her voice rose with each word, a haunting desperation floating through the tone.

Dillon leaned forward and squeezed her hand. "I know what you're saying. But I have another idea for us. I'd like to go talk to the Bradshaws."

Her face went still as she seemed to process that thought. "Why do you want to do that?"

"Because Burt mentioned them, and he's right. Liam worked a case against that family that could have left them with a lot of resentment toward Liam. Maybe they're the ones who did something to Liam. And maybe that wasn't enough. Maybe they want to do something to Bella also. I think we should talk to them. I'd like to do it myself and not leave it to Chief Blackstone."

Erin stared at him a moment, her eyes glimmering with uncertainty, until finally she nodded. "Okay then."

He turned his gaze back Carson who stood in the doorway. "Do you think you can handle this?"

Carson nodded quickly. "I can do it. I know I can. Thank you for trusting me with this."

"We've been through all these drills before. I have total confidence that you'll be able to handle the situation. There are going to be a lot of teams out there searching today. I heard the park service put out a call for volunteers."

"Is anyone from Boone's Hollow coming out to help?" Erin rubbed her throat as if anticipating the worst.

"I'm not sure. But I know that people from the surrounding counties are coming. There should be a good group there to scour the woods."

"I am grateful for that at least." But her voice still sounded tight.

"While they handle the search and rescue operation side, we're going to talk to the Bradshaws and see if we can get any answers from them. I know we don't need to waste any more time here. I think this is our best option."

She stared at him a moment before nodding. "Then let's do it."

NINETEEN

Erin stepped from the hallway, still gripping her phone and reeling from the conversation she'd just had. When her phone had rung, she'd stepped away for privacy.

"Erin?" Dillon glanced at her as he stood at the front door waiting.

"Bella's best friend, Gina, just called." Erin rubbed her temples as the conversation replayed in her mind. Each time made her feel like she'd been punched in the gut.

"Is everything okay?" Dillon's forehead wrinkled as he stepped closer to her.

"Gina told me the police brought her in this morning for questioning. And she..." Erin drew in a shaky breath.

Dillon squeezed her arm. "It's okay. Take your time."

Erin gulped in a deep breath, trying to keep

her composure even as panic raced through her. "She told them Bella and I had been fighting lately and that I'd threatened to kick Bella out of the house."

Dillon continued to wait for her to finish, no judgment on his face. "Okay…"

She squeezed the skin between her eyes. "Bella and I have been fussing with each other recently, but it's just been the normal type of parent-teenager argument that happens. I did tell Bella that she needed to straighten up, but I had no intention of kicking her out or putting her on the street."

"So why did Gina tell the police that?"

"She said they kept pushing her. She said that she knows I'm a good mom, but the police kept pushing her to say something. Finally, she cracked." Erin closed her eyes, willing herself not to cry. There had already been too many tears.

And tears wouldn't help her find Bella. This was no time to feel sorry for herself. That would only waste time.

Concern filled Dillon's gaze. "Is that all she said?"

"She said she had the impression the police were going to bring me in for questioning again." Her voice trembled as unimaginable scenarios raced through her head. "They're going to arrest me, aren't they?"

"A verbal argument between you and Bella doesn't give them probable cause for arresting you."

Her gaze met his. "But I already have a target on my back. Who says these guys are going to play by the rules?"

"I know what you're getting at. You think they're looking for an excuse to put you behind bars."

"They've wanted to for over a year."

"We are not going to let them arrest you," Dillon finally said.

She shook her head. "I don't see how we can stop them."

"Right now, we're just going to keep doing what we'd planned on doing."

"Are you sure?" Tension threaded through her voice.

Dillon nodded. "I'm sure. Now, let's keep going. We don't have any time to waste."

Erin nodded, but her thoughts still raced.

How could Gina have said that? How could the police have kept pushing her until she did? Now she was just going to look even more guilty than she already did. People in this town were going to have another reason to hate her.

Just once Erin had thought things couldn't get worse, that's exactly what they seemed to do.

Dillon typed the Bradshaws' address into his GPS. The family consisted of three brothers—Bill, David and Samson. Each was a powerhouse in his own way, and people in town knew it was best not to mess with them. Mysterious incidents would happen if they did—slashed tires, smashed car windows, unexpected fires.

But nothing could ever be traced back to the family, though everyone knew they were guilty.

Their place was a good thirty-minute drive from here.

As he headed down the road, his thoughts continued to race.

He wondered how Carson and Scout were doing. He wanted to call to get an update, but he didn't want to interrupt the operation, either. They would contact him if they needed to.

Meanwhile, he hoped that he wasn't leading Erin right into the line of fire. He knew this family wasn't safe, but he also knew he couldn't leave Erin alone.

In an ideal situation, he would have brought backup. But since Dillon wasn't officially a cop anymore, there was no one to ask to come with him. Plus, with the suspicion that had been cast on Erin, he wasn't sure how many of his friends would be willing to help. Especially if it meant risking their career.

"Tell me about when you adopted Bella," he started.

Erin glanced up, her gaze still looking strained. "I was friends with Bella's mom in high school. Her name was Stephanie. She didn't have a good home life and had gotten involved with drugs and more of the party crowd. But I used to always help tutor her in math, so we became friends, I suppose."

"Okay…"

"We lost touch for a long time," Erin continued. "Then Bella ended up in my first-grade class. I knew her mom was having a hard time. I could see it in her eyes, and I'd heard through the grapevine that social services was on the verge of taking Bella away from her."

"What happened next?" Dillon glanced in his rearview mirror, feeling like they were being followed again. He didn't tell Erin. Not yet.

"One day, out of the blue, I got a phone call from Stephanie. She was hysterical, and I could tell that she was on something. She asked me if I would take care of Bella for her. She said she needed to go get help."

"And you said yes?"

"I did. I love Bella. Even when she was just my student, I thought she was a great kid. So I told Stephanie that her daughter could come live with me and Liam."

"What happened next?"

"Stephanie tried to get help, but it was too

late. She called me again and said she wanted me to adopt Bella, that she couldn't handle being a mom anymore. I tried to convince her to keep getting help, tried to encourage her that she could change. But Stephanie wouldn't listen and insisted that Bella needed to be with me, that I was a good person. I didn't know what to say."

"What did Liam think?" Dillon asked.

"At first, he was supportive. I think it made him look good that we'd taken in a little girl and helped her out. He liked the accolades he got because of that. In fact, when I mentioned to him that we could adopt her, he was all in favor at first. I don't think he really realized what he was saying yes to."

"Was Bella troubled?"

Erin sucked in a deep breath. "She'd had a rough past, and of course that affected her. It would affect anybody. But we were working through it. Bella isn't a bad girl by any means. Like I told you earlier, it's mostly her anxiety that gets to her."

"And eventually Liam realized that and held it against you?"

Erin nodded. "His fuse just kept getting shorter and shorter. I thought he might change if we had a child in the house. That it would awaken a gentler side of him. I was wrong. He only escalated and things got worse and worse."

"But Liam never hurt Bella?"

"No, I made sure of that," Erin said. "Bella was the reason I ultimately decided I couldn't stay with Liam. I couldn't risk him ever hurting her."

"What about Bella's birth mom? Did she totally disappear after that?" Dillon glanced in his rearview mirror again. Somebody was definitely following them. The vehicle maintained a steady distance behind them.

Erin rubbed her throat as she stared out the window. "Once the adoption was finalized, I never saw her again. I still wonder what happened to her. Where she ended up. If she is still alive."

"How about Bella? Does she ask about her?"

"She did when she first came to live with me. But over the years, the questions faded.

I'm sure she still thinks about her mom, though. Who wouldn't? But perhaps she got tired of hearing the same answers."

"I'm sorry to hear that. I can only imagine that must have been really hard on her."

"It was. I hate to see a child go through that. I did what I could—I'm *doing* what I can— to give her a good life. But in so many ways, I feel like I failed her also."

He shot a quick glance at her, curious about her words. "What do you mean?"

"Maybe I should have said no to the adoption. Part of me feels like I took her from one bad situation and I put her in another." Her voice caught.

"But you did everything that you could to protect her." He understood the guilt—even if he thought the guilt wasn't justified. It just added more pain to an already difficult situation.

"Bella is gone now. Whether she ran away or if she was abducted, either way, it kind of feels like I fell down on the job, doesn't it?"

Dillon squeezed Erin's hand, wishing he could offer her some more comfort. "I know it might feel like that now, but you have to know that's not the truth."

Before she could respond, Dillon looked into the rearview mirror again and saw that the car was still there.

Somebody was definitely following them.

And it was time to end this.

Now.

Erin sucked in a breath as the Jeep suddenly skidded to a halt. The back of the vehicle fishtailed until the Jeep blocked the road.

Her eyes widened. What was happening?

She knew by the stiff set of Dillon's jaw that something was wrong.

When she glanced back, she saw a red pickup behind them.

They were being followed again, weren't they?

Not only that...but that truck looked familiar. Where had she seen it before?

"Stay here," Dillon growled.

He grabbed his gun before stepping from the Jeep and storming toward the person following them.

"Get out of the car with your hands up."

Erin held her breath as she waited to see what would play out.

After several minutes, there was still no movement.

This wasn't good. What if the driver opened fire? Or what if that person decided to ram them?

There were so many unknowns.

A moment later, the truck door opened.

Her heart throbbed in her chest.

Then a familiar face came into sight.

That's why Erin had recognized that truck. It was Arnold, Liam's brother.

She lowered her window so she could hear what happened next.

Arnold raised his hands in the air as he scowled at Dillon. "Let's talk this through."

"You didn't seem interested in talking when you were following us just now."

Erin climbed from the Jeep and stood behind Dillon. "What are you doing, Arnold? Do you have Bella?"

He pulled his head back in shock. "Why would I have Bella?"

She started to lunge toward him when Dillon stuck his arm out to stop her from going any closer.

"Why would you do this to me? Why would you take her?"

"I didn't take Bella," Arnold said. "Why would I do that?"

"Why are you following us right now?"

He sneered. "Isn't that obvious?"

"Clearly, it isn't obvious," Dillon said. "Now, why don't you give us some answers before I take you in?"

"Last I heard, you weren't a cop anymore."

"That doesn't mean I can't march you down to the police station so they can question you there. Don't think that I won't do it."

Arnold stared at him another moment, as if trying to ascertain if he was bluffing.

He must have decided that he wasn't because he finally spoke. "I didn't take Bella. I may not like you, but that doesn't mean I want to hurt the girl. Besides, everybody knows *you're* the one who did something to her."

Fury sprang up inside her, and she fisted her hands at her sides. "Arnold, you have to know me good enough to know I'd never do something like that."

His gaze locked with hers. "You did something to my brother."

Erin's throat burned as emotions warred within her. "You know that I didn't do anything to your brother. He was the one who hurt me."

Arnold's gaze darkened. "Then you just had to exact revenge on him, didn't you?"

"If you knew he was hurting me, why didn't you try to stop him?"

Arnold's shoulders bristled. "It wasn't my place. He said you got what was coming to you."

The burning in her throat became even greater. More tears welled in her eyes, but Erin held them back. She wouldn't give Arnold the satisfaction of seeing her cry.

"You're saying that you're not the one who took Bella?" Dillon's voice sounded hard and unyielding.

Arnold crossed his burly arms over his chest. "I didn't take Bella. That's ridiculous."

"And why are you following us now?" Dillon continued.

"Because I need to let Erin know she's not going to get away with this."

Realization dawned on her. "You're the one who's been sending me those text messages, aren't you?"

Arnold said nothing.

"You probably left that message painted on the front of my house also. And you're the one who threw that bottle bomb at us."

His nostrils flared. "I just want to see justice for my brother."

Dillon bristled beside her. "Threatening Erin isn't the way to do it."

She heard the anger—and protectiveness—simmering in Dillon's voice.

"I can't let her get away with it," Arnold growled as he glowered at them.

"I think you know, if you look deep inside yourself, that Erin isn't guilty of this," Dillon said. "Now, you're just hindering our search for Bella. You're hindering our search for an innocent sixteen-year-old girl who's probably been abducted. I hope you can live with your-self knowing that."

Arnold's gaze darkened again, but he said nothing for a few minutes. "I didn't do it. I have chronic obstructive pulmonary disease. You know I do. There's no way I could have carried out a plan like this. Besides, I was at a doctor's appointment in Asheville the day she disappeared."

Erin let his words sink in. That seemed provable enough.

But she still didn't like this man and didn't want him around. He was dangerous in his own way.

"If I see you around one more time, I'll be calling in all the favors I'm owed by the local law enforcement community." Dillon's voice sounded hard, like he wasn't someone to be questioned. "Don't think I won't do it. Do you understand?"

Arnold stared at him a moment before nodding. "Understood."

TWENTY

As they continued down the road, Dillon's pulse raced.

That man had a lot of nerve.

He wished he had the power to arrest him now. But they had more important matters to attend to. At least they now knew where those texts had come from along with the message on Erin's house.

Was Arnold the person who'd tried to run them off the road? Dillon's gut told him no. He'd thought that vehicle had been gray, and this man's truck was clearly a bright red.

Was he the one who had been in the woods? Who'd thrown the bomb?

"Are you doing okay?" He glanced at Erin.

Certainly, that whole conversation had shaken her up. It would shake anybody up.

She crossed her arms over her chest and shrugged. "Hate can do horrible things to people, can't it?"

"Yes, it can. I'm sorry you have to be on the receiving end of that."

Before they could say any more, Dillon's phone rang and he saw that it was Rick.

He hit the talk button, and the man's voice came out through his Jeep's speakers.

"Hey, Rick," Dillon started. "I'm here with Erin."

"Good. I can talk to both of you at once. There are a couple of updates I want to give you."

"What's going on?" Dillon waited, hoping for good news. But by the sound of his friend's voice, he wasn't sure that's what they were going to get.

"First, I just heard through the grapevine that Blackstone got a warrant to search Erin's house. He's probably going to take her computer and look for any evidence that she may have done something to Bella."

A muffled cry escape from Erin beside him.

Dillon frowned.

Another hit. How many more could she take?

"I also wanted to let you know that we got our official report from the medical examiner," Rick said. "The body that we found in the forest that day wasn't Liam's."

Erin gasped. "What? But the necklace…"

"It appears that somebody placed the necklace on the body. Maybe they did that just to throw us off."

"Then whose body was it?" Dillon asked.

"It belonged to a drifter named Mark Pearson. He went missing about fifteen months ago, not long before Liam went missing."

"How did he die?"

"It looks like he had a head injury. He was known for his involvement in drugs. That probably played a role also."

"Thanks for letting us know."

"Where are you now?" Rick asked.

"We're headed to see the Bradshaws and give them a visit."

"The Bradshaws? Be careful. They're not a family that you want to mess with."

Dillon's spine tightened at his friend's reminder. "I know. We'll watch our backs."

"If you need anything, let me know."

Dillon rubbed his jaw. "We will."

Erin's heart continued to race.

That body wasn't Liam's.

She still didn't have confirmation about whether he was dead or alive.

Sometimes, she just wanted an answer. Living with the unknown was too hard. At least if that had been Liam's dead body, she could put that part of her life to rest.

Now the possibility still remained that he was alive and out there somewhere.

Otherwise, things didn't make sense. Why would Liam have run away and hidden? For this long, too?

He was the type of person who loved people. He loved being the center of attention, and he wasn't the type who wanted to hide in a cave for an indefinite period of time. If he was doing that, he was desperate.

"What are you thinking?" Dillon's voice snapped Erin from her thoughts.

"I'm just trying to process all this."

"I understand."

"I can't believe the police are searching my house. Then again, I shouldn't be surprised." She rubbed the sides of her arms, suddenly feeling chilled.

"That's pretty standard in investigations like this," he said. "They always look at family first."

She shook her head, feeling half numb inside. "They're not going to find anything—unless somebody has planted something."

A sick feeling filled her gut. What if that were the case? Given everything else that had gone wrong, it did seem like a possibility. Somebody wanted to make her look guilty. This could just be another way of making her suffer.

"Let's not think about that. Let's wait and see what happens next."

She nodded, knowing she had no choice but to do exactly that.

Dillon pulled up to a house that was set off the road on a long lane. The log cabin, which looked almost like a lodge, had probably cost a pretty penny. Yet despite its massive appearance, the place wasn't well cared for. Too much trash was outside. Too many cars in the driveway. The lawn was too unmanicured.

As Dillon parked the Jeep, he turned to Erin. "Stay here while I talk to them. Whatever you do, don't get out."

Erin heard the warning in his voice and knew that he wasn't messing around.

But before Dillon could even open the door, gunfire rang through the air.

"Get down!" Dillon shouted.

They ducked below the dash as more bullets filled the air.

The Bradshaws were shooting at them.

Dillon could feel the adrenaline pumping through him.

He drew his own gun as he tried to figure out his next move.

He hadn't come this far to leave now. But he didn't want to put Erin in danger, either.

At a pause in the rounds of ammunition, Dillon raised his head. "I'm just here to talk!"

"Who are you?" one of the men yelled back.

"My name is Dillon Walker."

"What do you want?"

"I want to talk to you about Liam Lansing."

Silence stretched as he waited for the man's response.

Finally, the man said, "What do you want to know?"

"We want to know if you know what happened to him," Dillon said.

"Why would I know that?"

Dillon raised his head again. "Look, can we just talk? Without any guns?"

The man was silent another moment until he finally said, "Come up to the porch. But don't try anything or there will be consequences."

Dillon glanced at Erin again. He didn't like this and knew things could go south fast. "Listen, if anything happens, I want you to get behind the wheel and drive away as fast as you can. Do you understand?"

"Dillon…" Her voice cracked with worry.

His gaze met hers. "I mean it. I don't want you getting hurt. Bella is going to need you when she's found. Do you understand?"

Erin stared at him, emotions filling her gaze until she finally nodded. "Okay."

He climbed out and started toward the house.

As he did, he felt the tension thrumming inside him. Would this guy do what he had said? Criminals in general couldn't be trusted. Dillon hoped he wasn't walking into an ambush.

Bill Bradshaw stepped onto the porch, a shotgun in his hands. The man was in his fifties, with short silver-threaded hair and a hooded gaze.

He was well seasoned in his life of crime. He had whole networks of people working for him. Even though his home wasn't well maintained, it probably had cost more than a million dollars. Money wasn't an object for him. His drug business clearly paid well.

"What do you want to know about Liam?" Bill asked, a cold, hardened look in his gaze.

"His daughter is missing," Dillon said.

"I heard that. But I still don't know what this has to do with me."

"We're wondering if there's a connection between their disappearances."

Bill raised a shoulder and scowled. "Why would I know?"

"I heard that you have some bad history."

"He tried to arrest us, if that's what you're talking about." Bill's eyes narrowed. "Do you think I killed him?"

"We have no idea what's happened. But we wonder if Liam's disappearance is somehow connected with the disappearance of his daughter Bella. Bella's mom is worried sick, and I'm just trying to find some answers."

The man stared at him, his eyes narrowing even more. "You were one of those state cops, weren't you?"

The fact that this man knew that fact didn't surprise Dillon. Bill probably studied all the local police departments so he would know what he was up against in case something tried to come between him and his drug operations.

"Is there anything you know that might help us to find him?" Dillon asked.

"I don't want that guy found. I don't help cops."

"So you don't know anything?"

He continued to stare at Dillon.

He *did* know something, Dillon realized. But what?

"Now I need you to get off my property," Bill growled.

"Just a few more questions—"

"I need you to get off my property now."

Dillon stared at him and heard the warning in his voice.

But as he took a step back, more gunfire rang out.

He spotted one of the Bradshaw sons in the window—holding a gun.

Dillon needed to get out of there. Now.

TWENTY-ONE

Erin heard more bullets being shot and gasped.

She'd promised Dillon she'd leave at the first sign of trouble.

A promise was a promise.

But she couldn't leave him here. He'd be a sitting duck.

Quickly, she climbed into the driver's seat, trying to remember everything she could about driving a stick shift. She'd learned in high school, but that seemed like a long time ago now.

With her hand on the gearshift and foot on the clutch, she managed to get the Jeep into first gear.

She nibbled on her bottom lip and had to make a quick split-second decision.

Leave or help Dillon?

It was a no-brainer.

Releasing the clutch and pressing the accelerator, she charged toward the house in front of her.

She wasn't leaving Dillon behind.

As she got closer to Dillon, she slowed and opened the door. "Get in!"

Dillon's eyes widened, but he dove inside.

Before he closed the door, she did a quick U-turn and charged back down the lane.

As she did, a bullet pierced the back glass, shattering it.

But as long as she and Dillon were okay, that was all that mattered.

Keeping her foot on the accelerator, Erin shifted the gears again and drove as fast as she could to get away from the house.

She had to keep Dillon safe and she had to stay alive in order to help Bella. Those were her only two goals right now.

She turned back onto the street just as Dillon sat up and jerked on his seat belt.

"I told you to leave," he muttered.

"I did leave. I just picked you up first."

He shook his head before a laugh escaped.

A laugh? That wasn't what she had been expecting.

"You have a lot of guts, Erin. Don't let anybody ever tell you that you don't."

"I'm glad you made it out okay. But did you find out anything in the process?"

His eyes softened with concern. "Not really. They definitely know something, but the Bradshaws aren't going to share what it is."

"I remember overhearing a few things and thinking that Liam and this family were mortal enemies. Maybe *they* did do something to Liam."

Dillon leaned back. "Did the police ever look into them?"

"It's hard to say." Erin let out a sigh. "What now?"

"Let's head back into town, and maybe stop to grab a quick bite to eat in the process."

"But first, we're going to switch seats. No way am I going to try to drive this up the mountain."

He grinned. "I think you're doing a pretty good job."

"Then I need to stop while I'm ahead."

* * *

What Erin had done was risky. But it may have saved his life. If she hadn't had the nerve to drive by and pick him up, he could be dead right now.

What she had done had also meant that she could have been hurt. And that wasn't okay.

As she pulled off onto the side of the road, Dillon climbed out to switch seats with her. As their paths crossed behind the Jeep, he paused and grasped her elbow.

"Thank you." His voice came out throatier than he had intended.

Her cheeks turned a shade of red. "It's no problem. You would have done it for me."

"You're right. I would have."

Their gazes caught and, for a moment, all he wanted to do was lean down and press his lips into hers.

The urge surprised him. It was so unexpected.

All of this was.

A search and rescue case had turned his life upside down once. Now it appeared that another case might turn his life upside down again. Maybe it wouldn't be in a bad way this time.

Right now, he needed to concentrate on finding Bella.

Dillon cleared his throat, wishing it was that easy to also clear his thoughts.

"It's cold out here," he finally said. "We should probably get back in the car."

Erin stared up at him, something swirling in the depths of her eyes. She felt it, too, didn't she? Dillon had a feeling she was in the same boat that he was.

She wasn't looking for a relationship. It sounded like the one relationship she'd had in her life had put her through the ringer.

He swallowed hard again before stepping back. "Let's get inside. You've got to be hungry. Maybe we'll grab a quick bite to eat and then we can keep looking."

Erin seemed to startle out of her daze as she nodded at him. "Sounds like a plan."

They both climbed back into the Jeep, and he took off down the road.

As he did, his thoughts raced.

It seemed as if they could rule out Arnold as

being involved. But Dillon would guess that whoever was behind this wasn't a stranger. This seemed too personal for that. It wasn't about money; when a stranger was involved in a crime like this, it was usually for financial reasons. Erin clearly did not have much cash.

So if they ruled out Arnold, who did that leave? Could the Bradshaws be involved? It seemed like there was a good chance, but what would their motive be?

There was still a lot they needed to figure out.

He stared at the road in front of him. There was another town near, one adjacent to Boone's Hollow. Dillon knew of a diner where he and Erin could grab a quick meal before they continued looking for more answers.

Part of him was looking forward to spending more time with Erin and getting to know her even more.

What would the future hold when this was over?

Dillon didn't know. But he did know that the most important thing was that when this was all over, Bella was safe.

* * *

Erin glanced at the restaurant in front of her. Surprisingly, she'd never been here. She wasn't much for going out to eat, not when she could cook things on her own. Besides, that was the way Liam liked it, and she'd tried to respect his wishes.

"They have great BLTs if you're interested," Dillon said.

"That sounds great." As if in response, Erin's stomach rumbled. She was clearly hungrier than she'd thought. Maybe all this danger had worked up an appetite.

It had certainly worked up questions within her.

As soon as they stepped inside, the scent of comfort foods filled her senses. Was that roast beef? Gravy? Maybe even chocolate?

She couldn't be sure, but whatever the scents were, they were alluring.

"What do you think?" Dillon glanced at her. "Do you want to sit down for a few minutes and regroup? Or should we get this to go?"

Erin glanced at her watch. "I suppose that if we can eat something quickly, we can stay."

It was always good to recalculate and figure out the next step. Plus, this wasn't Boone's Hollow. Maybe she could grab a bite to eat without everyone scrutinizing her like they did back in her hometown.

The waitress led them to a seat in the corner and handed them laminated menus. But Erin didn't even need to look at it. She would get a BLT just as Dillon had suggested. That selection sounded good.

She glanced around the outdated but friendly-looking restaurant before turning back to Dillon. "Do you eat here a lot?"

"Not really. But on occasion I want a meal that reminds me of Grandma's. When I do, this is where I come."

Erin wanted to engage in simple chitchat, but her heart wasn't in it. Not when so much was on the line.

Instead, she said, "Can we review everything we know?"

"Of course." Dillon shifted across from her.

Erin's mind raced through everything as she tried to sort through her thoughts. "So this is what we have so far. Bella disappeared when she went to school three days ago. Her car was found in a parking lot near a trailhead. A body was found on the trail, but it belongs to a drifter and doesn't appear to be connected to the case other than the necklace found on the corpse."

"Correct," Dillon said.

"Meanwhile, Arnold sent me threatening texts as well as left a message painted on the front of my house," she continued. "He also threw that bomb."

"Also correct."

"One of Bella's shoes was found twenty miles away, at a different section of the park. Five hundred feet from that, her other shoe was found. In the meantime, there's been no real contact."

"That sounds accurate."

She frowned and nibbled on her bottom lip for a moment. "Somebody's also been trying to run us off the road, watching us from the woods, they've shot at us, and that man was in my room last night."

Dillon reached across the table and squeezed her hand. "Unfortunately, all of those things are correct. Someone certainly is weaving a tangled web."

"Yes, they are. And when you put it all together, what do you have?"

"That's the million-dollar question. Who could possibly be behind this?"

His question hung in the air.

Erin heard the door jangle open behind her and glanced over her shoulder.

The person who stepped inside made her eyes widen.

She pulled away from Dillon's grasp and stared at the woman.

"Erin?" Dillon said from across the table. "Do you know that person?"

Erin nodded, her thoughts still reeling. "That's Stephanie. Bella's birth mom."

TWENTY-TWO

Dillon felt himself bristle as Erin stared at the woman who'd stepped into the restaurant.

He had a feeling he knew who this woman was.

Stephanie—Bella's birth mother. The two looked like each other and this woman was in the right age range.

As if to confirm his gut feeling, Erin muttered, "Stephanie?"

He was right. So what was Stephanie doing there?

He tensed as he waited to see what would happen next.

The woman's gaze latched on to Erin. Stephanie had obviously known Erin was there and had come to find her. But how had she known that? Had she been following them?

His muscles tightened even more at the thought.

The woman ambled toward their table now.

She had straight blonde hair that was pulled into a sloppy ponytail, and wore faded jeans and an oversized sweatshirt. The gaunt expression on her face, combined with her thinning hair and dull eyes, seemed to indicate a history with drug abuse—in Dillon's experience, at least. Her red-rimmed eyes showed grief...and maybe more.

"Erin..." She paused at the edge of their table, her hands fluttering nervously in the air.

"Stephanie." Erin's eyes widened with surprise. "What are you doing here?"

"I... I needed to talk to you. I heard what happened and..."

"Of course." Erin scooted over in the booth and patted the space beside her. "Have a seat. Let's talk."

Stephanie carefully perched herself there, but her body language seemed to indicate she could run at any minute. Her muscles were stiff. Her gaze continually drifted back to the window. Her fingers flexed and unflexed.

Dillon leaned forward to introduce himself. "I'm Dillon, a friend of Erin's. I'm trying to help her find Bella."

Stephanie frowned and nodded. "I know. I've been keeping an eye on things ever since I heard the news about Bella. I know that probably sounds strange, and I don't want to come across as creepy. I just didn't know what to do or if I should approach the two of you or not."

Erin reached over and squeezed the woman's arm. "We're doing our best to find Bella. I promise we are."

Stephanie used the sleeve of her sweatshirt and rubbed beneath her eyes as if wiping away unshed tears. "I know you are. I know that the scuttlebutt around town is that you may have done something to Bella. But I know that's not the truth."

"I would never hurt her." Erin's voice caught.

"I can't believe people would say that you would. I know you love her."

Erin placed a hand over her heart as relief filled her gaze. "I can't even tell you how relieved I am to hear you say that. I know you trusted me with your daughter, and I'd never want to let you down."

Stephanie sniffled and stared out the window before drawing in a shaky breath. "Giving Bella up was a hard decision. But I know that it was the right one, even with everything that's happened."

"So why did you come find me now?"

Stephanie ran a hand over the top of her head. "I want to do whatever I can to help. I don't just want to sit back and pretend like this doesn't affect me."

"You haven't heard anything, have you?" Dillon asked. "Or seen anything?"

"No. I wish I had something to offer you. But I don't."

Disappointment filled his chest cavity, even though he'd expected that response. "I understand."

"We need to find her." Stephanie's voice cracked as her gaze connected with Dillon's.

"What if she's hurt? What if someone took her?"

"That's what we're trying to figure out," Dillon assured her.

"Or what if she's just like me? What if she ran, trying to escape all her problems?" Her expression pinched with pain.

Her words hung in the air.

Her questions were valid. There were a lot of variables in place here.

And time was quickly running out.

As Erin and Dillon headed back down the road, Erin's thoughts wandered.

On one hand, it was a relief to know that Stephanie didn't blame her for what had happened. That Stephanie thought she was a good mother. That she didn't regret her decision to let Erin adopt Bella.

On the other hand, the fact that Stephanie had shown up now of all times made Erin cautious. She hadn't seen the woman in years. Stephanie had smelled slightly of alcohol and cigarettes. And she'd looked so nervous.

Was that because Bella was missing? Or was there more to the story?

"That was surprising," Dillon said beside her, almost as if he could read her thoughts.

"You can say that again."

"I hate to ask this, but I feel like I need to. Do you think Stephanie could have anything to do with Bella's disappearance?"

Erin blinked as she processed his question. "I don't think Stephanie's the violent type, if that's what you're asking."

"No, but do you think there could be more to this?"

The implications of his question hit her. "Wait…you think that maybe this is all a scheme? That Stephanie wants Bella back, so she snatched her?"

Dillon shrugged. "It makes sense, and it wouldn't be the first time that something like that has happened."

Erin swung her head back and forth. "I just can't see her doing that."

"The timing is uncanny."

"I can't argue with that. But I just don't

know… I don't want to think she's capable of doing something like that."

"I just want you to be careful," Dillon said. "It's hard to know who to trust with everything that's happened."

"I know. And I appreciate your concern."

Silence stretched between them for a moment.

Finally, Erin glanced back over at him. "Where are we going?"

"I need to swing by the house and check on the dogs since Carson isn't there. It will only take a few minutes."

She nodded. "Of course. Have you heard any updates?"

"Unfortunately, no. But everyone is still searching. That's good news."

Erin stared out the window, trying not to be bothered by the conversation. But she knew Dillon had to ask about Stephanie's sudden appearance. He wasn't the type to skirt around the fact that Stephanie could have ulterior motives.

A few minutes later, they pulled up to his house. Erin scanned the buildings and woods around them to make sure there were no signs of danger. Everything looked clear.

For now.

After all that had happened, they had to be careful. Danger could be hiding around any corner.

Dillon parked his Jeep and turned to her. "Let's do this. And then we'll figure out our next steps."

Erin nodded, but tension still coursed through her.

She was growing more and more anxious by the moment.

Dillon escorted Erin inside so she could freshen up. Once he'd secured the doors and made sure everything was safe, he headed outside to the kennel to check on the dogs.

As he did, Erin slipped into the bathroom and stared at herself in the mirror. This experience seemed to have aged her. She didn't remember dark circles beneath their eyes before. Didn't remember looking so tired or her hair looking so dull.

She leaned against the sink and closed her

eyes. *Dear Lord, please help Bella right now. Help us to find her. Lead us to her. Please. I'm desperate, and I'm sorry for those times that I've doubted You. Because right now, I know I'm not going to get through this without You.*

After muttering, "Amen," Erin opened her eyes and splashed some water in her face before wiping it dry with a towel. She'd promised Dillon she would wait inside until he came back just as a precaution.

As she wandered toward the living room, her phone buzzed.

She looked down at the screen and the words that she saw there made her blood go cold.

If you want to see Bella alive, meet me at the Buckhead Trailhead. Come alone. Or else.

Her heart pounded in her ears. Was this for real?

Erin knew that it was. The number wasn't the same one Arnold had used to send her those other threats.

This had most likely been sent by the person who'd abducted Bella.

Erin nibbled on her bottom lip as she thought through her options. Clearly, she didn't have a vehicle here. Her own car was in the shop, the tires being replaced.

Maybe she should just tell Dillon. Maybe he could help her figure something out.

The instructions were explicit. The sender had said Erin had to come alone.

And the penalty if she didn't?

Bella would be hurt—or worse.

It was a risk she couldn't take.

But how was Erin going to meet anyone without a vehicle?

As the question fluttered through her mind, her gaze fell on the keys Dillon had left on the kitchen counter.

The keys to his Jeep.

She swallowed hard before glancing out the window to where the dog kennel was located.

Dillon was still inside. Still out of sight. Still occupied.

Erin thought about her decision only a moment before grabbing the keys.

She could slip outside and borrow his Jeep.

Dillon would be angry with her. Erin knew he would be. Really angry.

But she had to do this for Bella.

She had no other option.

Before she could second-guess herself, Erin started for the door.

She prayed this was the right choice.

TWENTY-THREE

As an unexpected noise sounded in the distance, Dillon rushed from the kennel.

As he did, he saw his Jeep pulling from the driveway.

His Jeep?

He darted toward his house, praying that Erin was safe.

After searching inside, he knew she was gone.

Realization spread through him.

Erin had taken his Jeep, hadn't she? Why would she do that?

Was she setting out to find Bella on her own?

The thought of her doing that sent concern ricocheting through him.

There had to be more to this story.

But Dillon didn't have time to ponder that.

Right now, he needed to catch her and find out what was going on.

He darted to his desk and pulled the drawer open. After riffling through paperclips and notepads, he finally found what he was looking for.

The keys to a truck he kept inside his barn.

He grabbed them before sprinting outside, yanking the barn doors wide, and climbing into the old truck.

After a few tries, the old truck engine finally rumbled to life. He eased through the open doors and made his way to the end of his driveway, he headed to the right, the same direction Erin had traveled.

But a few minutes later, when he reached a T in the road, Dillon realized he had no idea which direction she'd gone.

He contemplated his choices for a minute.

If he went to the left, it would lead him to the national forest where Bella was last seen.

If he had to guess, that was the direction Erin had headed.

Dillon jerked the wheel that way. As he did, he prayed—prayed that Erin was safe. That she would use wisdom. That God would protect her.

What could have happened to lead her to do something like this? Whatever it was, certainly Erin didn't realize what kind of situation she might be getting herself into right now.

Most likely, she was headed directly into danger. Whoever had taken Bella wouldn't stop until they got what they wanted. Dillon feared that what this person wanted was to make Erin suffer more and more.

It looked like Erin might be giving them that opportunity.

Now the challenge would be figuring out exactly what part of the national forest she might have headed toward. The place was large—500,000 acres—with uncountable trailheads. There was no way Dillon would be able to cover them all.

He had to figure out what he was going to do...and fast.

Erin felt the sweat across her brow as she headed down the road.

She prayed she was making the right choice. Prayed she wasn't making a bad situation worse.

What if she was playing right into the hands of the person who'd taken Bella? She knew there was a good chance she was.

But she'd sacrifice whatever necessary if it meant Bella would be safe.

She wiped her forehead with the sleeve of her sweatshirt before shifting gears as the Jeep climbed higher up the mountain.

It had been a rough ride. But she was doing okay.

Now she just needed to make it up this mountain.

And find the Buckhead Trail.

She should have looked up an address before she'd left, but she hadn't thought about it. She'd had to leave right then before Dillon stopped her. She'd had no time to waste.

Dillon…she frowned. She hadn't realized until now just how much she truly cared about that man.

But she did.

Even though it was crazy that her feelings

had grown so quickly in such a short period of time, that's exactly what had happened.

Dillon had been a rock for her. He'd cared about her when no one else had. And he hadn't doubted her story.

She wiped beneath her eyes.

Please, Lord, keep him safe. Don't let my decision hurt him. Help him forgive me.

She muttered an amen and then pulled herself together. Right now, Erin had to concentrate on Bella. Everything else she would deal with later.

What would the person who'd sent her the text do when Erin arrived? Take her to Bella? Kill her on the spot?

She had so many questions, so much that didn't make sense.

There were too many possible players in this scheme, and Erin didn't know which one might be behind this.

Whoever it was wanted to make Erin pay. She just didn't know what mistakes this penance was for.

Her hands gripped the wheel, white-knuckled. The mountain road was steep, and as she traveled to a higher elevation, the air became cooler. The road became icier.

You can do this, Erin!

She gave herself a mental pep talk. But the higher she climbed, the more her anxiety grew.

She should have told Dillon. Coming alone had been a bad idea. With every turn of the wheel, that seemed more and more clear. But there was no going back now. Erin doubted she even had any phone reception at this point.

More sweat beaded across her skin.

Finally, she spotted a sign on the side of the road.

Buckhead Trail.

It was only a mile away. She was getting closer.

She continued up the mountain, shifting gears and praying she could figure this out.

Finally, she reached the parking area for the trail.

She was here.

Erin let out a breath, even though she knew her trouble was probably just beginning.

The person who'd texted her had said for her to come alone. It was too late to change her mind now.

She'd followed the instructions and played by the rules.

Now maybe she could get Bella back.

She parked the Jeep and sat there a moment, her heart racing.

What next?

She glanced at her phone, but it was as she'd expected. She didn't have any reception.

How would she get her next set of instructions?

She leaned back and waited, her heart pounding in her ears.

Waiting would be the hardest part, especially if she started to second-guess herself.

As another car pulled into the parking lot, she sucked in a breath. Who else was here?

Her eyes widened as the vehicle came into focus.

It was a police car.

The cops were here?

Had they tracked her down so they could arrest her?

She pressed her eyes closed.

No.

Not now.

Not when she was so close.

Dear Lord...what am I going to do?

As she saw the door open and someone step out, she braced herself and tried to figure out how to handle this situation.

With every mile that went past, Dillon's worry grew.

Where had Erin gone? What had happened to make her do this?

Dillon only prayed he found her in time.

So far, he'd checked out every road that pulled off from this main one. But the task was tedious and taking too much time.

If only he knew where Erin was.

If he had more time, he could search his Jeep's GPS to see where the vehicle was located. But to do that he would need to go back to his house. For now, he would keep searching in his truck.

There were entirely too many pull-offs in

this area. Working this way would take for-ever. But he had little choice right now.

He studied each of the various trailhead signs as he passed, wondering if Erin may have decided to go search by herself. With her ankle being sprained and conditions being what they were, it sounded like a terrible idea.

Plus, he'd just heard while checking on his dogs that another snowstorm was headed this way. The last thing Erin needed to do was to be stuck on this mountain during a storm in her present condition.

He had to admire her determination as a mom. He knew that mothers were protective of their kids, and Erin had proven that to be true.

Dillon hoped there was a good solution for the situation, one where Bella would be res-cued and Erin would be okay.

He shook his head as he pulled onto an-other lane branching from the main road that wound through the mountains.

Erin should have told him what was going on. She should have never left on her own.

Just as those thoughts raced through his head, he spotted a vehicle in the distance.

His breath caught.

Was that his Jeep?

He pressed the accelerator harder as he headed toward it. Quickly, he pulled up behind it and then rushed to the front doors. He already knew what he would most likely find inside.

He was right.

Nothing. No one.

Erin wasn't here.

He bit back a frown.

He glanced around at the trees surrounding him.

Where had Erin gone?

As he stepped back, he spotted another set of tire tracks in the space beside the Jeep.

Erin had met somebody here.

But who?

Could Arnold really be guilty? Was he working with someone to teach Erin a lesson?

Or what about Stephanie? What if she really was involved?

Or there was always the Bradshaws. They had a long history of crime and violence.

He wouldn't put anything past that family.

It almost seemed like there were too many possible suspects.

There was no way Dillon would be able to track down all these people on his own.

He was going to need to call in backup.

As soon as he got phone reception, he would talk to Rick and find out what his friend could do to help.

Because something was majorly wrong here.

And if Dillon didn't get to the bottom of it soon, he feared Erin may not make it out of this situation alive.

Erin felt her throat tighten as she sat in the back seat of the police cruiser. She'd tried to explain that she couldn't leave. Tried to convince the officer that this was a mistake, that she was innocent.

But Officer Hollins hadn't listened.

Instead, she'd been placed in the back of the police car like a criminal.

Panic fluttered up inside her as the officer backed out and started down the road.

"How did you find me?" Her voice squeaked as the words left her lips.

"We've been watching you." Hollins glanced back at her. "Be glad I'm the one who finally tracked you down and not Blackstone. He's furious, and he has a major chip on his shoulder."

"He's had a chip on his shoulder for a long time." Erin shifted and glanced out the window.

As she did, more panic rose in her. How was she ever going to find Bella now? Her one opportunity had slipped away. She hated the helpless feeling swirling inside her.

"Hollins, you've got to listen to me." She leaned forward so he could hear the desperation in her voice. Her argument hadn't worked the first time, but maybe it would now. "If you don't let me meet the person I was supposed to meet, they're going to do something to Bella."

"What do you mean?" Officer Hollins glanced back at her in the rearview mirror.

"I got a text saying I had to meet whoever

had taken Bella at that location. If I'm not there, I don't know what's going to happen to her."

He continued to stare at the road ahead. "I can send an officer out."

"You can't do that. It had to be me." Her voice came out higher pitched and louder with each word.

"I told the chief that I would bring you in. He'll figure something out."

"You know that's not true. You know he thinks I'm part of this." Despair bit deep into her.

"You're just going to have to trust us."

But that was part of the problem. Erin *didn't* trust them. It was why she'd had to take matters into her own hands.

Erin squeezed her eyes shut. She desperately wished that Dillon was there right now. He would know what to do.

But she'd made the decision to go without him, and now she had to live with it.

She hoped this wasn't the biggest mistake of her life.

She slowly opened her eyes again, trying

to regain her focus. "What are you going to do with me?"

"I'm going to take you into the station for questioning. The chief said he found something on your computer."

Alarm raced through her as questions collided in her mind. "On my computer? There was nothing on my computer."

Had Erin been set up again? When would the hits stop coming?

"I'm just telling you what I heard," Hollins said. "I'll do everything I can to make sure Blackstone handles this in the right way."

At least Officer Hollins had picked her up. At least he was one of the good guys.

But there was so little positive Erin could see in this situation.

As Hollins turned off the street onto another road, Erin's spine straightened. "This isn't the way to the police station."

"I just need to make a quick stop first."

"A quick stop? Where?"

"You'll see."

But as Hollins said the words, a bad feeling grew in Erin's gut.

There was more to the story, wasn't there?

The truth nagged at her, but she didn't want to face it. Didn't want to think she could be right.

Instead, she braced herself for whatever would happen next.

TWENTY-FOUR

As soon as Dillon got reception, he called Rick and gave him the update. Rick promised to keep his eyes open and to alert the other park rangers that Erin might be missing. He also told Dillon there were no updates out on the trail and that the teams were going to head back soon.

It was a double set of bad news.

Before he ended the call, Dillon asked one more question. "Is Blackstone with you?"

"No, he's not out here today," Rick said. "He said he's manning the station. Why?"

"I'll explain later."

Dillon knew exactly where he needed to head next. He had to talk to Blackstone and let him know what was going on. Even if the man didn't take him seriously, there was no way Dillon could find Erin on his own. He needed help.

As he continued down the road, Dillon made a few more phone calls. He let his colleagues with the state police also know what was going on so that everybody could have their eyes open for Erin.

A bad feeling brewed in Dillon's gut as he thought about the possibilities of what had happened.

What if the person Erin had met in the parking lot was the same person who had taken Bella?

It was clear this person wanted to make Erin suffer. If Bella's abductor had been able to finally snatch Erin, maybe this would fulfill the last step of his plan.

Yet there were other things that didn't make sense. The person behind this had the opportunity to grab Erin after breaking into Dillon's house. Why hadn't he? Maybe he had some kind of weird timing he wanted to follow.

It was hard to always predict how criminals

thought. But in this case, this guy obviously had some type of agenda.

And Erin was at the center of it.

Dillon's gut clenched as he thought about it.

Finally, Dillon arrived at the police station. He quickly threw the truck into Park before hurrying inside. He bypassed the reception area and barged right into Chief Blackstone's office.

The man looked up at him and narrowed his eyes when he saw Dillon standing there.

"Can I help you?" Blackstone's voice sounded tense with irritation.

"Erin is missing."

His eyebrows flickered up. "Is she missing? Or did she sneak away to go check on Bella?"

Anger surged through Dillon. "You know Erin's not responsible for this. You just want to make her pay because Liam disappeared."

"You don't know what you're talking about."

"It's as plain as day that that's the case. I think somebody may have taken Erin. Most likely the person who took Bella."

Blackstone tapped his finger on his desk. "Why would they want both of them?"

"Clearly, it's because someone has some type of agenda. I need your help."

Blackstone shrugged. "I'm not sure what I can do. Most of my guys are out on the trails right now, looking for Bella. If Erin had just told us where she had taken her..."

Dillon slammed his hand onto the chief's desk. "You need to listen to me. Somebody took Erin and Bella, and we've got to find them before it's too late. Do you understand that?"

The chief stared at him for another moment. "I hear what you're saying."

"And what are you going to do about it?" Dillon hated to speak to the chief like that, but being nice wasn't cutting it with this man. He had to let him know he meant business.

Blackstone rose from his seat. "I'll let my other guys know what's going on, and they can be on the lookout."

At least that was something. But Dillon needed more. "Can you try to trace her cell phone signal?"

He stared at Dillon a moment, and Dillon

braced himself for whatever he was going to say.

But finally, Blackstone nodded. "Let me see what I can do."

As Hollins pulled off onto a side road, Erin's heart went into her throat.

"Where are you taking me?" she demanded. Her fingers dug into the seat beneath her as tension curled her muscles.

"It's like I told you. I just need to make a quick stop."

"Hollins…"

"Stop asking questions." His voice hardened.

As soon as she heard his words, Erin realized her worst fears were true.

Hollins was part of this somehow, wasn't he?

She leaned toward the plastic divide separating them. "You don't have to do this."

He didn't bother to look at her. "I don't know what you're talking about."

"I thought that you were my friend."

One of his shoulders tensed, rising slightly as he sat there. "You did wrong by Liam."

Wait... Hollins was doing this to honor his friend? Was that what this was all about? "Hollins...you don't know this whole story. You only know what Liam told you."

"You adopted Bella and then you kicked Liam out of the house. You took everything he'd worked so hard for. Liam tried everything to get you back."

"There's more to that story," Erin rushed to insist.

She glanced at the door handle, wanting to grab it and yank it open. But she knew the door was locked, and she couldn't open it from the inside.

There was no way out of this car.

She tried to push down the panic that wanted to bubble up inside her.

"I'm sure you're going to say he treated you badly," Hollins said. "That's what people always say."

"But Liam *did* treat me badly. I'm not even just talking about yelling at me. He hurt me, Hollins."

His jaw tightened. "He would never do that. He's a good man."

"Whatever you think you need to do right now, you don't have to do it," Erin told him, praying she might be able to convince him to change his mind.

"Yes, I do."

Erin swallowed hard, trying to think through ways she might convince him to change his mind. No good ideas hit her. Maybe she needed more information first.

"Are you the one who broke into Dillon's house and threatened me?"

He finally glanced over his shoulder and shrugged. "I wanted to send you a message."

"Why not just kill me there and get all of this over with?"

"Kill you?" His eyes widened. "You think that's our goal?"

Erin didn't miss the fact that he'd used the word *our*. Who else was a part of this? "What else would you want to do?"

"Plenty. You'll see. You're asking too many questions."

"Hollins…"

"Enough!" He sliced his hand through the air. "Enough talking. Anything else you want to know, you're just going to have to wait. Understand?"

Erin leaned back in her seat and stared at the forest as they traveled deeper and deeper into the woods.

How could Hollins be involved in this? Did he really want to make Erin pay this badly for what he perceived as a slight against his friend?

How was she going to get herself out of the situation? Especially considering the fact that she wouldn't be able to run, not with her hurt foot.

Hollins pulled to a stop at the end of the lane.

There was nothing in front of them.

They were miles and miles into the heart of the Pisgah National Forest, she realized. Clearly out of cell phone range. Where nobody else would be around for miles and miles.

Nausea gurgled in her stomach.

There was no one out here to help her, she realized.

Erin was going to have to rely on her own skills if she wanted to get out of the situation alive.

As promised, Blackstone had pinged Erin's cell phone, but it was out of range. Instead, Dillon had tried to follow the tire tracks away from that parking area. But in the lower elevations, the snow had faded and so had any tire tracks.

He'd only been probably ten minutes behind Erin, however. So if someone had picked her up, Dillon would have passed them—and he hadn't passed anyone on his way up the mountain.

The questions only made his temples pound harder.

There was only one way he could think to find her. It was a long shot. But it might work.

Dillon called Carson and told his nephew to meet him at the parking area where his Jeep had been found.

Normally, in situations like this, search and

rescue dogs could follow a scent on foot. But considering the treacherous mountain road, the fading daylight and approaching storm, that wouldn't be safe.

Instead, Dillon had grabbed a piece of clothing Erin had left at his place and then met Carson and Scout near the Buckhead Trailhead.

As soon as he saw Scout, he squatted on the ground and rubbed his dog's head. "You ready to work?"

Scout leaned into his hand.

"I need you to find Erin," Dillon continued. "Can you do that?"

Scout raised his nose as if he understood the question.

Without wasting any more time, Dillon let Scout sniff Erin's sweatshirt.

A few minutes later, the dog raised his nose into the air and sniffed. Scout began pulling Dillon back toward the entrance of the parking area.

Dillon knew the chances were slim, but he was going to give it a try.

With Carson driving, Dillon would sit in

the front seat with Scout. He'd put the window down and let Scout reach his nose out.

They slowly took off down the road.

Dillon hoped the dog would remain on the scent.

They crept back down the mountain. Dillon knew the next turnoff wouldn't be for another mile, but as they passed a section of woods, Scout began to bark.

Carson tapped the brake. "What do you want me to do?"

Dillon peered between the trees. "It looks like there's a service road right here that's just barely big enough for a vehicle to go through. The way the tree branches fall in front of it, it's nearly impossible to see from the road."

"I didn't notice it," Carson said.

"Let's see what happens. Turn here."

Carson did as he'd said, and they pulled down the narrow lane.

Just as Dillon had thought, the space was barely wide enough for them to fit through, and some of the overhead branches scratched the roof of his Jeep. Dillon would worry about that later.

Slowly, they continued along the gravel lane.

It was possible that Erin and whoever had taken her had gone down this lane before Dillon arrived. It was probably the right distance away that Dillon wouldn't have seen them.

His heart pounded harder. Maybe he was onto something.

Because he desperately wanted to find Erin.

In the short amount of time they'd known each other, he'd realized there was something special about her. He needed to find her and tell her that. He needed to stop holding on to the hurts of his past relationships and open himself up to more possibilities for the future. Possibilities with Erin.

There was a lot that needed to happen first.

Starting with finding Erin and Bella.

The task nearly felt insurmountable. But for Dillon, failure wasn't an option.

At the end of the lane, Carson pulled a stop. Right behind a police cruiser.

Carson nodded to the vehicle. "Do you know who that belongs to?"

Blackstone's face flashed in Dillon's mind. But Dillon didn't think the police chief could have gotten here in the time since they'd spoken. Was the chief working with somebody? Had he sent one of his guys here to take care of business?

It was a possibility.

In other circumstances, Dillon would call in the car to see who it belonged to. But out here, he had no phone reception.

Scout barked out the window at the car.

He was still on the scent.

That meant Erin had been here recently.

"We're going to have to go the rest of the way on foot," Dillon said.

Carson nodded beside him. "I want to help. Just let me know what I need to do."

Erin nearly stumbled down the trail as Hollins gripped her arm. He wanted her to move faster than she possibly could.

The trails were too steep. Too slippery. Her ankle was too weak.

He didn't care about that. All he cared about was that she kept moving forward.

So that's what Erin tried to do.

But every time she breathed a gulp of air,

her lungs hurt. It was so cold out here and the wind was only getting stronger and cooler by the moment.

If her gut instinct was right, a storm was headed this way. It was the only way to explain the sudden drop in temperature and why such a sharp breeze had stirred.

"Where are you taking me?" Her words came out between her gasps for air.

"I told you to stop asking questions."

"You're not like this," she told him. "You like doing the right thing. I can see it in your eyes."

His eyes narrowed. "Sometimes the right thing isn't black or white. Sometimes you have to go off course in order to do the right thing."

What did that mean? Could she break through to him? She was going to keep trying.

"I don't know what you think the right thing is, but I assure you that this isn't it," Erin said. "I'm innocent in all of this. I don't care what anyone has told you."

Blackstone's face flashed in her mind. He'd put his officer up to this, hadn't he? As vengeance for Liam's disappearance. It was the only thing that made sense.

"Just keep moving," Hollins muttered. "You're not going to change my mind on this."

"Do you have Bella?" Erin's voice cracked as the question left her lips.

"I said, no more questions."

"Please, I have to know. Is my daughter okay?"

He didn't say anything for a moment until finally blurting, "She's fine. Now, keep moving."

As Hollins shoved her forward, Erin nearly stumbled. Her knee hit the boulder in front of her and pain shot through her. She winced but didn't have any time to recover.

Hollins kept his grip on her arm and urged her down the path. "We don't have much time. The weather's going to turn bad."

"It's not too late to turn around now." Erin knew he wouldn't listen to her, but she felt like she had to try anyway.

"Keep moving," he grumbled.

With her shoulders tight, Erin did just that. She kept moving forward.

Finally, a cabin came into view. Yellow lights glowed from the windows.

The whole place looked like it was less than a thousand square feet, and there was no smoke coming from the chimney. It was probably cold inside.

But this was clearly where Erin was heading.

Hollins dragged her up the steps and opened the door.

The figure waiting for her there took Erin's breath away.

TWENTY-FIVE

"Liam?" Erin blinked as she stared at his oversized form.

He still looked basically the same, except now his blond hair had grown longer and a beard and a mustache covered part of his face.

But his eyes...they were still cold and calculating enough to send a shiver through Erin.

"Are you surprised to see me?" His words sounded full of malice as a mix of satisfaction and dark amusement mingled in his tone.

She tried to back up but Hollins caught her and pushed her forward. "I thought you were dead."

"That's the point. Everybody is *supposed* to think that I'm dead."

Hollins shut the door behind her, and the brisk wind disappeared for a moment.

They couldn't use the fireplace. From a distance, the smoke would have drawn too much attention. Instead, piles of blankets were on the couch and there was an electric heater. If she had to guess, this place was solar-powered.

"Why do you want people to think you're dead?" Erin stared at Liam, still unable to believe he was standing in front of her.

"It's a long story," he muttered.

Her gaze wandered around the room, looking for any signs of Bella. Looking for any signs of what was going on here.

Nothing caught her eye.

"Why did you bring me here?" Erin drew her gaze back up to meet Liam's. She needed answers. Would he offer her any? "Why have you done all of this?"

He stepped closer and ran his finger down her arm. "You're here because you're mine. If you thought that you were just going to divorce me and walk away and I was going to pretend like none of this happened, then you were sadly mistaken."

She cringed and tried to back up. But Hollins was still there, holding her in place. "So you're just going to live out the rest of your days here? Pretending that you're dead?"

"Maybe. But for now, I'm safe here."

Her breath caught as more realizations raced through her mind. "You got yourself in some type of trouble, didn't you?"

His gaze darkened. "That's not important. What's important is that you're here now. Our little family is back together."

"Where's Bella?" Erin demanded.

He nodded at Hollins. Hollins took his cue, walked over to a door off to the side and opened it. A moment later, Bella nearly tumbled to the floor.

As soon as Bella spotted Erin, tears flooded her eyes. She drew herself to her feet and darted toward Erin. "Mom!"

"Bella!" Erin threw her arms around her daughter as tears flooded her eyes. "I was so worried about you."

"I'm so sorry, Mom," Bella breathed. "I should have never gone without you."

Erin had so many questions for her daughter, but now wasn't the time to ask them.

Now was the time to figure out how she and

Bella were going to get out of this seemingly no-win situation.

With an arm still around Bella, Erin turned back to Liam. "Now that you have us both here, what are you going to do with us?"

His eyes sparkled with some kind of unspoken plan. "I thought we could just settle down and live like the perfect little happy family for a while."

Was he serious?

There was no amusement in his gaze. That realization terrified her.

"There's nothing happy about the situation," Erin reminded him.

He nodded at the window. "There's a snowstorm coming, so you might as well get comfortable. We have a lot of catching up to do."

A sickly feeling trickled in Erin's gut.

Liam really had lost his mind, hadn't he? Who exactly had he gotten himself into trouble with—enough trouble that he'd had to hide away from the rest of the world?

Liam had been perfectly content to let people think that Erin had done something. It was one way of making her pay for divorcing him.

Erin had to figure out how she was going to get out of the situation.

She had no time to waste.

Dillon and Carson followed the trail as Scout pulled them along.

Erin had definitely come this way. Dillon had no doubt about it.

As they walked, a smattering of freezing rain fell between the branches above them. Conditions were only going to get worse and worse.

They had to find her and soon.

Dillon looked at his phone. He still had no reception. Thankfully, he'd told his state police officer friends as well as Rick where they were heading. Maybe they would know to follow this trail just in case they needed some backup here.

Dillon paused Scout on the path and sucked in a breath.

Carson nearly collided into them. "What's going on?"

Dillon put a finger over his lips. Then he pointed to the ground. "Look at all the footsteps here. If Erin came this way, she either had an army with her or people were following her."

Carson's eyes widened. "But there were no other cars in the parking lot."

His nephew raised a good point. "There's probably more than one way to get to this trail. Either way, we need to be on guard. We don't know exactly who we're up against here."

Carson nodded and they continued, quietly making their way down the trail. They had to watch their steps to make sure they had no more injuries. That was the last thing they needed to slow them down.

Dear Lord, please be with Erin now. Keep her safe. Protect her. Bella also. Guide our steps and help us to find them.

The deeper they headed into the valley, the rockier the trail became. They weren't moving as quickly as Dillon would have liked, but he reminded himself that slow in actuality meant fast. Being careless would only make them trip up, and he couldn't afford to do that.

As something in the distance caught his eye, he paused.

"It's a cabin," he muttered.

Carson stopped beside him. "Do you think that is where Erin is?"

"It's my best guess."

Scout would get a nice reward later for leading them here.

Dillon kept his hand raised in the air, motioning for Carson to remain still. Then he scanned everything around him.

He spotted three men hiding in the brush in the distance. If he wasn't mistaken, they had guns in their hands—guns that were aimed at the cabin.

Best he could tell, they hadn't spotted him, Carson or Scout yet.

Dillon would have to be careful as he planned his next move.

Erin still held Bella as they stood facing Liam.

"I still don't understand why you're doing this," Erin said.

"You don't have to understand." He sneered at her. "You just need to be pretty."

Erin narrowed her eyes. "You're the one who called and told the police chief that my car was on the trailhead on the day Bella disappeared, weren't you?"

His grin was answer enough for her. "I wanted them to scrutinize you. I wanted you to feel the heat."

"I'm guessing you sent Hollins into the woods near Dillon's place? He was the one who broke into Dillon's home." She glanced at Hollins as he stood guarding the door, his face expressionless.

"I just wanted to send you a message. I understand you and Dillon were getting pretty cozy."

She shook her head. No doubt, that had only upset him more. But Dillon was the last thing she wanted to talk to Liam about.

"Everything still doesn't make sense," Erin continued. "You had opportunities to snatch me, if that's what you needed to do. Why go through all the trouble of taking Bella and then sending me those threats?"

"I've always liked playing games with you."

She sucked in a breath. His words were true. He'd tested her, left dishes in the sink just to see if she'd wash them, rearranged drawers to see if Erin would straighten them.

And if she hadn't met his expectations... then she'd paid for it.

So Liam had taken Bella, knowing that would make her suffer the most. Then he'd sent Hollins to keep an eye on her. To threaten her. To let her know there was more to come.

Enjoying her mental anguish was just a small gratification for him.

The thought made disgust roil in her stomach.

Erin turned her thoughts back to the present. She surveyed the cabin, trying to find any means of escape.

But even if she and Bella managed to get away, there was no way the two of them could navigate these mountains. It would be dark soon. Freezing rain hit the roof. And Erin's ankle and leg throbbed.

She looked at Liam again. "What are you going to do with us now?"

"Right now, I want you to sit down and be quiet for a few minutes. There's been way too much talking for my comfort."

Erin took Bella's hand and led her to the couch.

"Hollins, keep an eye on them," Liam ordered.

"Yes, sir."

Liam disappeared into a different room while Hollins stood guard with his arms crossed over his chest. As he did, Erin turned to Bella.

"How are you?" she asked, looking Bella over. "Did he hurt you?"

With tears rimming her eyes, Bella shook her head. "No, he just scared me."

"How did he even lure you away?"

"Someone left me a message on a piece of paper saying that I needed to meet at the trailhead, that your life was in danger. But when I got there, I saw Officer Hollins. He told me he was going to take me to you."

Erin's eyes flickered to Hollins, and she scowled.

"Instead, he led me down the trail. Liam

was waiting for us. Hollins left me with him, and Liam insisted I had to come with him. He had a gun. He made me walk down these trails and over cliffs until we got to this cabin."

Erin's heart lurched into her throat as she imagined what Bella had been through. "I'm so sorry that happened to you. We've been looking hard for you."

"I know you have. I knew you wouldn't give up."

Erin wrapped her arms around Bella and held her. "You have no idea how worried I was."

"I love you, Mom. I'm sorry you're here with me now, but I'm glad to see you at the same time." She sniffled.

Erin didn't let go. "I know, sweetie. I know."

"What are we going to do?"

Erin glanced around the cabin again. "I wish I knew. But we'll figure out something. We just need to be brave."

"I wouldn't do that if I were you," Hollins muttered.

He'd clearly been listening to their conversation.

"How did you get involved with this?" Erin asked. "I always thought you were a good cop."

"Liam trained me," Hollins said. "He told me what you were like. He told me about the conspiracies against him. Told me I couldn't believe anything."

"Conspiracies about what?"

"About—"

Before he could finish, the window shattered.

A bullet had flown through that window.

Someone was outside, and they were shooting at them.

It couldn't be Dillon. He wouldn't be that careless.

If Liam and Hollins were inside, then who could possibly be behind the gunfire now?

TWENTY-SIX

When Dillon heard the gunfire, he knew he had to spring into action. There was no time to waste.

He pushed Carson back and handed him Scout's lead. "Stay here."

Carson nodded and ducked behind a boulder.

Crouching low, Dillon moved closer to the cabin. He gripped his gun, prepared to use it if necessary.

Aiming carefully, he took his first shot. He hit one of the men in the shoulder.

The man let out a yelp before falling to the ground.

One down. Two more to go.

But he knew those two remaining guys could do a lot of damage.

Especially now that they knew Dillon was there.

Just as the thought raced through his mind, a bullet split the bark on the tree beside him.

Dillon was going to have to get closer. Those guys were going to breech that cabin, and there was no telling what would happen then.

As he crept closer, another bullet flew through the air.

Before he could duck out of the way, pain sliced his arm.

Dillon let out a gasp.

He'd been hit.

"Get behind the couch!" Liam yelled. "Now!"

Erin heard the anger in his voice and rose. Wasting no time, she shoved the couch from the wall and pulled Bella back there with her.

More bullets continued to fly.

As they did, Liam pulled out his gun and crouched beneath the window.

Things began to click in Erin's mind.

Liam was hiding because he'd made someone mad, wasn't he? Likely, it was the Bradshaws.

Now he had no choice but to hide out or they were going to kill him.

It made sense.

"Mom..." Bella's wide eyes stared at her.

Erin squeezed her hand and held her close. "Just stay low."

More bullets flew.

What was going to happen if the gunmen outside got inside? Would they all be goners?

It was a good possibility. At least Liam appeared to want her alive for a little while.

As more bullets flew, Erin heard someone gasp. She raised her head enough to see Hollins drop to the floor.

He'd been hit in the chest. Blood filled his shirt.

She swallowed back a scream.

Just as Erin thought things couldn't get worse, someone burst through the door. When she heard Liam mutter something beneath his breath, she knew they were in trouble.

The gunman was inside.

Dillon glanced at his biceps.

The bullet had grazed his skin.

He might need a few stitches, but otherwise

he was going to be okay—other than the pain from where the bullet had sliced into his arm.

As he saw the gunmen moving toward the cabin, Dillon crept closer. One man approached the door while the other stood back.

Dillon got in place behind the tree and then aimed his gun. When he pulled the trigger, the bullet hit the one man in the shoulder and he fell to the ground.

Now it was just the gunman at the door.

And whoever else was inside.

As Dillon heard another bullet fire, a scream sounded from inside.

His heart pounded harder. Was that Erin? Was she okay?

He had to get closer.

He darted toward the back of the cabin. There was a window there, and he should be able to see inside.

Remaining low, he crouched beneath it and peered inside.

Liam stood there, his back to the window.

He was alive.

Dillon sucked in a breath.

And the man was probably behind most of this chaos.

Dillon would deal with it later.

He continued to scan the interior of the cabin. He spotted two people huddling behind the couch.

Erin and Bella...

They were okay!

Relief filled him at that realization.

Thank you, Jesus!

But he had other issues to address first... starting with the fact that Bill Bradshaw stood in front of Liam with his gun raised.

The Bradshaws were also involved in this. They'd probably been hunting Liam this whole time. Somehow, when Erin came here, she must have led them right to Liam.

While Dillon didn't care what happened to Liam, he couldn't risk something happening to Erin and Bella.

"You thought you were going to get away with this," Bill muttered.

"How did you find me?"

"I've been following that state cop and your ex-wife ever since they came to my house," Bill said. "I figured they might lead me to you, and I was right. Now, I need you to put your gun down."

Liam's nostrils flared. "That's not going to happen."

He turned his gun toward Erin. "Then I'll shoot them first."

"I don't care if you shoot them," Liam said. "But you're not walking away from here alive."

"You've been trying to find evidence to take my family down, haven't you?" Bill said. "But you got in with the wrong people. You're not going to get away with what you've done."

Dillon continued to listen. What exactly had Liam done?

"I didn't do anything," Liam insisted.

"You stole money from us! Money you found during a police operation. Then you tried to bribe us."

Liam said nothing.

But suddenly everything made sense.

Liam had tried to blackmail a crime family. They'd probably put a bounty on his head, and he'd been forced into hiding.

Except, Liam was too much of a narcissist

to simply disappear. He'd wanted his old life back—one way or another. That's why he'd come after Erin and Bella.

In the blink of an eye, Bill shifted his gun toward Liam and pulled the trigger.

Erin screamed.

Liam collapsed on the cabin floor.

Bill had shot him, Dillon realized.

"Now it's your turn," Bill grumbled, his gaze on Erin.

Wasting no time, Dillon rose, aimed, and pulled the trigger.

But not before Bill also fired his gun.

Erin huddled with Bella behind the couch, praying they'd stay safe.

When she glanced up, she spotted someone peering in the window.

Was that… Dillon?

Her breath caught.

It was! He was here!

He was okay.

Thank you, Jesus.

But what about everybody else? What was happening inside this cabin?

Erin dared lift her head even more.

When she did, she saw both Liam and Bill Bradshaw on the floor. They'd both been shot.

"Stay here," she whispered to Bella.

Quickly, Erin darted from her hiding space. Both men were still alive, their chests rising as they breathed. If they were alive, that meant they were still dangerous.

She kicked the gun away from Liam before he could grab it from the floor. Instead, she darted across the room and snatched the weapon herself. She needed to have it on hand, just in case.

At the thought, Bill raised his head and moaned.

Her eyes rushed to the ground.

His gun was still at his fingertips. One move and...

She knew she didn't have time to grab the gun.

Before she could figure out what to do, men in SWAT uniforms invaded the cabin.

"Police! Put your hands up!"

The state police. They were here.

The gun fell from her hands, clattering on the floor as relief filled her.

Erin nearly collapsed to the floor herself.

But before she could, arms caught her.

She looked up and saw Dillon there.

As the police took over the scene and a paramedic checked Bella, Dillon folded her into his embrace.

This was finally all over.

She melted in his arms.

"Are you okay?" Dillon muttered.

"I am now that you're here."

He pulled her closer. "I was so worried. You shouldn't have left without me."

"I know. It's a long story. I'll explain later."

Dillon's gaze was full of warmth as he pulled away just enough to lock gazes with her. He gently placed a kiss on her cheek, one that assured her everything would be okay.

"We'll have time to talk later," he said. "I hope we'll have a lot more time for talking together."

A grin spread across her face.

Erin liked the sound of that.

She glanced over at Bella again. Right now, she had to concentrate on her daughter.

But she and Dillon would definitely finish this conversation later.

TWENTY-SEVEN

"This is like my dream come true!" Bella hurried from dog kennel to dog kennel so she could meet all the canines at Dillon's place.

As she did, Erin and Dillon stood back and smiled as they watched her.

Seeing her bounce back after such a horrific ordeal was wonderful. Erin had been anxious that what had happened would set Bella back—and in ways, it had. The healing process would take time.

But overall, Bella was doing so well.

A month had passed since Bella had been rescued. Liam and Bill Bradshaw were now behind bars, as were their henchmen. In the midst of the media blitz about everything that had happened, Blackstone had been in the hot seat over his handling of the case. That had eventually led to the mayor firing him and offering Dillon the job. Dillon had turned the position down.

He liked what he was doing here apparently. As he should.

He was a great dog trainer, and the work he did was valuable.

Dillon wrapped his arm around Erin's waist and pulled her closer.

"I think Bella likes it here," Erin murmured, still watching her daughter. They'd purposely waited a while before bringing Bella here. They hadn't wanted to rush things.

But, so far, Bella and Dillon had really hit it off. Seeing Dillon come to their rescue had only helped their quick bond.

"I think she does, too," Dillon muttered.

Scout deserted the bowl where he'd been lapping up water and wandered toward them. As he did, Erin knelt on the ground in front of the canine. "And how are you doing today, boy?"

She rubbed his head as the dog leaned into her.

Thankfully, Scout hadn't been hurt in the

middle of the shootout. Carson had kept him safe.

"I think he likes you," Dillon said.

"You led Dillon to me, didn't you?" Erin murmured. "You helped save my life. Thank you, boy."

She'd already thanked the dog numerous times, showered him with attention, and even brought him some bones.

Erin gave Scout one more head pat before rising again.

As she did, Dillon caught her in his arms. He stole a glance over his shoulder as if checking to see if Bella was still occupied.

When he saw that she was, he planted a kiss on Erin's lips. "In case I haven't told you this yet, I'm so sorry about everything that happened. But I'm so glad this path led me to you."

Erin's heart warmed as she stared into his warm eyes. "Me, too. You've been a real godsend, Dillon Walker."

He leaned forward and kissed her again.

"I love you, Erin Lansing," he told her.

Erin grinned. "I love you, too."

"Am I going to have to tell you two to knock it off again?" Bella called from the other side of the building.

They laughed before turning to her, arms still around each other.

Bella strode toward them, her eyes on Erin. "It's actually nice to see you happy. You never looked like this when Liam was in your life."

Erin's smile faded. "You're right. I didn't."

Until she'd met Dillon, Erin didn't know what a good relationship could look like. She was so grateful God had brought him into her life.

She looked forward to their future together... a future complete with Bella and Scout.

* * * * *

Dear Reader,

Thank you so much for reading *Dangerous Mountain Rescue*. I hope you enjoyed getting to know Dillon, Erin and Scout as much as I did.

Like the characters in my book, have you ever been painted in a negative light? Have untrue accusations been thrown at you?

The Bible says in Colossians that God had rescued us from the darkness and brought us…redemption.

I love the word *redemption*. It means that we've been saved from sin or error. It means forgiveness.

Erin and Dillon both felt an oppressive sense of accusation throughout the story. Their pasts came with seemingly impossible burdens. But in the end, they overcame those obstacles and found the freedom they sought.

We can do that, too, when we rely on God and trust in His plan for us and our future.

Until next time!
Christy Barritt